"Savannah, alm[...]
we've had nothin[...]
weren't like this [...]

Savannah node[...]

"You seem so d[...]
have run-ins every day. And then [...]
you come in with someone else's clothes on,
dripping wet. I mean, who ever heard of someone
falling into the Avon?"

"Don't you believe me?" Savannah asked, her
voice rising.

"Shhh—do you want them to come out here?
Of course I believe you, but face it, it didn't
happen to anyone but you."

"What are you trying to say, Greg?"

"I'm saying it all wrong. When I saw you come
in with that English guy—"

"Philip?" Savannah asked cooly.

"Yeah, Philip. It's just that when you two came
in together, I got so jealous. I don't want you
going out with him. He looks at you in a way
that just makes me furious. And I just hate it
when the girl I'm going out with gets involved
in crazy escapades," Greg continued. "It's so
embarrassing."

"Savannah," Greg said, taking her hands in
his, "I really like being with you. Don't let Philip
or anything else get between us, okay?" Slowly,
he pulled her toward him and kissed her softly
on the lips. "Please don't get involved with him
in any more crazy schemes."

"I won't," Savannah promised, crossing her
fingers behind her back.

"That's my girl," he said, kissing her again.

Bantam Books in the SWEET DREAMS series. Ask your bookseller for any titles you have missed.

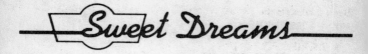

ACTING ON IMPULSE

Susan Jo Wallach

BANTAM BOOKS
NEW YORK • TORONTO • LONDON • SYDNEY • AUCKLAND

ACTING ON IMPULSE

A BANTAM BOOK 0 553 28463 0

First publication in Great Britain

PRINTING HISTORY
Bantam edition published 1991

Cover photo by Pat Hill

Bantam Books are published by Transworld Publishers Ltd.,
61–63 Uxbridge Road, Ealing, London W5 5SA,
in Australia by Transworld Publishers (Australia) Pty. Ltd.,
15–23 Helles Avenue, Moorebank, NSW 2170, and in New
Zealand by Transworld Publishers (N.Z.) Ltd., Cnr. Moselle
and Waipareira Avenues, Henderson, Auckland.

Made and printed in Great Britain by
BPCC Hazell Books
Aylesbury, Bucks, England
Member of BPCC Ltd.

*To Mom and Dad
with love*

Chapter One

"**S**avannah! What's the emergency? Why did I have to drop *everything* I was doing and come here?" Thea Tomaselli asked accusingly as she ran into her best friend's bedroom. She leaned against the door frame, out of breath.

Surrounded by clothes in different piles, Savannah Wheeler stood in the one clear patch—on top of her bed. "It suddenly hit me that maybe this isn't real. Maybe it's a horrible trick or a dream. Are we really going to England?"

"Couldn't you just ask me this on the phone?" Thea complained.

"No, I would only know it was true by looking at you—you couldn't lie to my face about something this important."

"It's only true if you can get your stuff packed and get on the plane."

"Oh, Thea! I'm so happy!" Savannah yelled, jumping off her bed and twirling her friend around. "Just imagine—thatched-roof cottages, winding cobblestone streets, hot scones with real cream, boys with English accents . . ." Savannah's deep blue eyes were alive with excitement.

Thea untangled herself from her friend's arms and stood up. "Savannah, there's no way you're ever going to be in England unless you pack, and pack soon. You're due at my house to eat dinner in less than an hour, and we leave tomorrow morning. I'd pack for you, but you'd probably hate what I choose." Thea grimaced as she surveyed the clothes on the bed. "You'd be so embarrassed, you'd never leave the hostel . . ."

Savannah shook her head, then grinned mischievously. "There's no way you could embarrass me. If necessary, I would even borrow Mr. Chiochi's clothes." Both girls laughed at the thought of Savannah wearing the vice principal's straightlaced, boring polyester clothing.

"All right, so nothing could keep you closed up in the hostel. But wouldn't you prefer to wear clothes that you look good in rather than something I might pick out?" Thea asked. "After all, Greg Edwards will be there. . . ."

Savannah's eyes opened wide and she jumped up. She began to search through her clothes, creating new piles. "Thea, can you believe it? I have to make the absolute best impression on Greg for the next two weeks, at least. What should I bring? What do I look best in?" Savannah stared at her clothes and then at her reflection in the mirror. "Why can't I look more like you? You look the way a girl is supposed to look." Savannah had always envied her best friend's golden blond, straight hair, round blue eyes, and glowing tanned complexion. "I've got this horrible red hair and freckles," she added with a wail.

"Savannah Wheeler, if I hear that one more time, I'm going to kill you. Your blue eyes and your wavy auburn hair are perfect for you. You always look so alive and vibrant. I couldn't imagine you any different. And your freckles are cute."

Savannah burst out laughing. "Alive and vibrant? Where did you get that from? Have you been reading *Cosmo* again, Thea?"

"Yes, I read it in that magazine," Thea replied haughtily. "And I immediately thought of you, if you must know."

"Thanks, Thea. You are the best, truest friend I could ever have," Savannah said, smiling.

"Don't get all mushy. You might not be *Glamour* beautiful, but you do have unusual looks. And that's appropriate, since I've known you since we were seven and I'm still never sure of what you'll come up with! But I wouldn't want you any other way," Thea added quickly, moving next to Savannah at the dresser mirror. She put her arm around her friend's shoulder.

"You know, that day in the playground was the luckiest day in my life." Savannah laughed as she thought of the day she had first met Thea nine years ago.

"We were seven years old," Thea began.

"And you were new and looked so clean in

your blue-and-white dress that it made me mad," Savannah continued.

"And so before you knew what you were doing, you threw that pail of water at me," Thea added.

"And you came charging after me with your fists."

"And you gave me a black eye."

"And you gave me a bloody nose!" Savannah cried. "And we were both sent to the principal's office—Mr. Chiochi."

"Who is *not* our pal," the two girls said together.

"But sitting out there, waiting for him, I realized that for a girl in a sissy blue dress, you had a great right punch," Savannah remembered.

"What was I supposed to do when you insulted my best dress? Fortunately, I have two older brothers who taught me how to fight," Thea reminded her.

"Yeah, well, Mr. Chiochi wasn't as impressed as we were. I think he had great hopes for you—you looked like such a good kid," Savannah said. "He knew from kindergarten that I would never be the ideal student. I was always too much of a tomboy."

"You know, my mother didn't think that was such a great day, either. Since then, I've never been the same sweet girl she always wanted. You have corrupted me, Ms. Savannah Wheeler, and for that I am eternally grateful."

"But old Mr. Chiochi isn't! I can still remember his face when he said, 'I'm surprised at you, Miss Tomaselli. You, Miss Wheeler, can never

4

surprise me. I dread to think of what you'll be like when you're older.' Well, if he didn't want to know me when I was older, why did he have to become our high school vice principal?" Savannah asked with a frown.

"I know," Thea agreed. "I wish he weren't coming on this trip with us."

"Oh, England! Greg! And I still don't know what to pack!" Savannah exclaimed.

"Let's start now, or we'll never make it to dinner in time," Thea commanded as she pushed all the clothes off Savannah's bed and dropped the backpack on the empty spot. Methodically, she picked up various items of clothing, and Savannah nodded either yes or no to them. Slowly, Thea filled the backpack with practical clothing, like jeans and sweaters, along with Savannah's favorite emerald green sarong skirt and her red, white, and blue cotton-knit sailor dress. When her job was done, Thea watched with satisfaction as Savannah put the rest of her clothes back in the closet.

"I don't think you need to worry about impressing Greg Edwards anyway. He's already noticed you and is definitely interested," Thea mused from Savannah's rocking chair.

"Do you really think so? I don't feel like the type he likes," Savannah admitted.

"We'll go over this one more time," Thea said rocking gently in the white wicker chair. "One: Whose idea was it to have our English class go to Stratford-on-Avon to see Shakespeare as he should be done?"

"Mine," Savannah answered meekly, smiling.

"Two: Who solved the problem of how to raise enough money, so we could go on the trip?" Thea continued.

"Me."

"Three: Who organized all the fund-raising activities?"

"Me." Savannah grinned.

"It is elementary, my dear Ms. Wheeler," Thea said, playfully wagging her finger at her friend, "that without you this historic trip could never have happened. And not only do you have the gratitude of everyone in our class, but also the admiration of a certain Greg Edwards."

"You *have* been reading romance novels!" Savannah exclaimed, clapping her hands.

"Please let me continue. This Mr. Greg Edwards —handsome, incredibly popular soccer star— likes Ms. Savannah Wheeler, girl extraordinaire. He volunteered to help you with all the fund-raising; he pays a lot of attention to you now; you two went out to dinner last week at Boston's coolest restaurant."

"I know you're right, Thea. But I'm scared. So far, when I'm around him, everything has worked out," Savannah said, walking to her dresser. She stared at herself in the mirror. "I haven't gotten in trouble for a long time. I know Chiochi is surprised. I am." She turned to face Thea and grinned. "There's going to be a time when my luck doesn't hold. So far, I've been able to be the way I think he wants me to be."

"Is that what you've been doing?" Thea asked.

"I've been wondering why you've seemed more like our favorite classmate Elaine Lacey than the Savannah we all know and love. I've missed your boycotting cooking class because the teacher buys California grapes or when you tried to start a shelter in the gym for all the homeless cats."

"I've been studying Greg, and Elaine is more the type of girl he seems to like," Savannah explained, her face serious. "That's what I mean when I said I've been lucky. I haven't made any big goofs around him, and I've been incredibly sweet, too."

"Savannah, if he wanted to go out with someone like Elaine, he would pick Elaine. Obviously, he doesn't. He likes you," Thea argued.

Savannah shook her head. "He likes the Savannah he's seen over the past few months, the one who can get things done. Not the one who is sometimes too loud and enthusiastic or clumsy. And he's going to get the Savannah that he likes. It's time for me to grow up anyway."

"If I didn't know better, I'd think I was talking to an alien in the body of my best friend," Thea said. "You never cared what people thought of you before. If Greg cares so much, maybe he's not the one for you."

"He is," Savannah said determinedly. "He's everything I've always wanted. He's smart and good-looking and is so right all the time. He never looks awkward or out of place. Thea, don't laugh, but he looks exactly like the prince I've always imagined. And he is as good as he looks.

7

If it means I have to calm down or change for him to like me, I will," Savannah finished, smiling as she remembered their dinner together.

"Instead of being so concerned about how you might not measure up to Greg, maybe you should think about whether or not *he's* good enough for *you*."

"What do you mean? There's nothing wrong with him," Savannah insisted, dropping the sweater she had just folded.

"No? If he's so wonderful, why do you feel you have to change in order to be with him? And I bet you haven't told him the real reason you want to go to England so much."

"Thea, you're the only one I trust not to laugh at me. It's just too private to tell Greg; we don't know each other well enough yet. But once we're going out, I'll tell him. That's what I want this trip to do—bring us closer together."

"Well, I think there's a good reason that you haven't told this 'perfect' boy about any of this." Thea stopped speaking when she saw Savannah's disappointed face. "I'm sorry. I could be wrong, Savannah. I don't know him; you're the one who's spent time with him, not me."

"Thea, I'm sure that once we're in England, he and I will get even closer and then I'll tell him about my grandfather. Even my parents don't know I remember all the stories he used to tell me as a kid and how I feel like I belong in England more than here," Savannah whispered. "I just know that this isn't going to be any ordinary trip."

Savannah smiled as she thought of her big, laughing grandfather and his boyhood stories about England. Ever since she could remember, she had longed to go to England and see all the places her grandfather had told her about.

"Well, all I want is an English lord," Thea said. "Actually, any Englishman would do as long as he has a gorgeous accent."

"All I want is Greg," Savannah declared. "He looks just like I imagine Heathcliff would look, with his dark hair and eyes. And his voice is so deep and romantic. He doesn't smile a lot, but when he does, he looks so beautiful."

"If I hear about Greg Edwards's perfection one more time again today . . ." Thea threatened, holding a pillow over Savannah. "I'm hungry, my mother's expecting us, and I still need to pack."

"Calm down. You would think that all I've done is talk about Greg Edwards for the past three months," Savannah said, laughing as she grabbed the pillow and threw it at Thea.

Thea groaned. "Why am I friends with you? What have I ever done to deserve this?"

"You just happen to be lucky!" Savannah laughed and stuck her tongue out at Thea.

Chapter Two

"Dad, the exit's over there," Savannah pointed out, practically climbing over the front seat to make sure her father didn't miss the ramp.

"Yes, Savannah, I see it. Why don't you just sit back and enjoy the ride? I promise to get you to your plane on time," Mr. Wheeler said, his voice betraying slight impatience.

"Thanks so much for driving us, Mr. Wheeler," Thea said. "My folks just hate driving to the airport."

"That's okay, Thea. Dad'll miss me when I'm gone and wish he was sweeter to me when he had the chance," Savannah declared.

"Savannah, you'll only be gone for two weeks. It's not as if you'll be gone forever."

"You never know, Dad. I might just meet someone who will beg me not to leave him—" Savannah started.

"What? And leave the perfect Greg?" Thea whispered, poking her friend in the side.

"Well, make sure you write us if that happens

so we don't make an unnecessary drive out to Logan Airport," Mrs. Wheeler replied dryly.

"Oh, Mom! You can't deny it. You'll miss me terribly," Savannah insisted, ignoring Thea's jibe.

"Luckily, sweetheart, we're saved from answering. Here you are," her father answered, laughing as he pulled the car up to the door of the international flights terminal. "Why don't you bring in your carry-on luggage and stand in line? I'll unload the rest from the trunk and bring them to you inside."

As Mr. Wheeler took the bags out of the trunk, Savannah and Thea headed for the check-in line.

"There you are! I'm not surprised that you two are the last ones to arrive," Mr. Chiochi said to them as he walked over, a clipboard in his hands and a whistle around his neck. He was wearing a familiar brown suit and shoes, although his crew cut seemed extra short for the trip.

"Hi, Mr. Chiochi," Thea said.

"Mr. Chiochi, the instructions were to be here by six, and it's only a quarter to now. We're early," Savannah protested.

"Girls, it's good to see you," Ms. Martin, their English teacher, quickly interjected, knowing Savannah and Mr. Chiochi's history. She was dressed in casual slacks and a sweater, her brown hair pulled back in a ponytail. "After you finish with your bags and tickets, meet us at Gate Sixteen. Mr. Chiochi, why don't we join

12

the rest of the students? These girls are fine here."

Shaking his head, Mr. Chiochi allowed Ms. Martin to lead him to the gate.

"I don't know, Thea. I think Chiochi and I might have some trouble in the next two weeks."

"Just let him talk and ignore him, Savannah," Thea advised. "Don't let him spoil this trip."

"I'll try," Savannah promised. "But he's always picking on me."

"Here you go, girls," Mr. Wheeler said, dropping their big backpacks on the ground next to them.

"Thanks, Dad."

"We thought we would leave now that everything is settled, if that's okay with you two. I did see Ms. Martin, didn't I?" Mrs. Wheeler asked.

"Yes, she and Mr. Chiochi went to the gate and told us to meet them there. We'll be fine, Mom," Savannah assured them.

"I'll miss you, sweetie," her mother said, hugging her daughter tightly. "Promise me you'll drop us a postcard, and call if you need anything."

"I will, Mom," Savannah whispered as her eyes filled with tears. " 'Bye, Dad."

Mr. Wheeler smiled and grabbed his daughter in a big bear hug. "Take care of yourself and have fun, Savannah-Banana," her father instructed her gruffly, and then surprised Thea by hugging her, too. "You have fun and don't break too many hearts."

13

Savannah and her parents hugged one more time and then they left, waving all the way to the door. Savannah turned to Thea, her eyes shining brightly. "Thea, we're on our way. We're actually going to England!" She grabbed Thea and gave her a big kiss.

"Sorry to interrupt such an emotional scene, but you two are next!" the airline employee called with a grin.

Blushing, the two girls presented their tickets and placed their heavy luggage on the scale.

A few minutes later the two friends headed toward the gate. Suddenly Savannah stopped abruptly in the middle of the long, wide corridor.

"Come on, Savannah-Banana, Chiochi will wonder what's taking us so long," Thea said.

"I can't go to England," Savannah said in a panicky voice, her face pale. "You'd better go on without me."

"What are you talking about?"

"Promise me you won't tell anyone. Ever," Savannah demanded.

"Of course I promise," Thea swore. "What's the matter?"

"Thea, I'm petrified of the thought of flying. I've never done it before. I've been putting it out of my head for weeks, hoping some miracle would happen. But just now, realizing that I have to get into a plane and be up in the air—I don't know if I can do it," Savannah explained, her hands shaking.

Thea led her to the plastic seats on the side of the corridor, and they sat down.

"We'll sit together, and you can hold my hand as hard as you like. I'll tell you stories, I'll even sing for you," Thea promised. "Besides," she added with a grin, "it would be too satisfying to Chiochi if you backed out now."

Savannah let out a deep breath. "You will hold my hand?" she asked. Thea nodded. "All right, but *please* don't tell anyone I was afraid. I don't want Greg to know how scared I am. I'm sure I'll be fine once we're in the air—I mean, I hope I will."

Quickly, they walked to Gate Sixteen, where they saw the rest of their classmates. Mr. Chiochi was writing on the paper on his clipboard, and Ms. Martin was talking with a group of parents who had decided to wait until the plane took off.

"Savannah, you made it!" She turned around and saw Greg standing behind her. Greg's dark brown hair was tousled just perfectly over his brow, and his brown eyes were warm as he smiled at her. Dressed in jeans and a white button-down shirt, his lean, athletic body had never looked better. "You look great," he said.

"Uh, thanks, Greg." Savannah found herself at a loss for words, something that only seemed to happen around Greg. She looked down at her black leggings and periwinkle blue oversize shirt. "Are your folks here?"

"No, they left after they dropped me off. Can you believe we're finally going? And it's all because of you. You've done such a great job."

Savannah blushed, but she smiled and turned

15

her head, hoping her hair would hide the color. "It was nothing," she said. "I'm sure anyone could have done it. I just happened to be the one this time."

"Well, I'm still impressed. Everyone knows it was you who really pushed and organized this trip," Greg said, moving closer to her.

"Mr. Edwards, Ms. Wheeler, please come over here, now!" Mr. Chiochi called to them.

"Geez, can't he ever call us by our first names?" Greg muttered to Savannah as they joined the group.

"Did you say something, Mr. Edwards?" Mr. Chiochi inquired, glaring.

"No, just that we're coming." Greg gave Savannah a quick grin when Mr. Chiochi turned back to his clipboard.

"Pay attention, people. Ms. Martin and I have assigned the seating on the aircraft, which I will now run down for you," the vice principal announced.

Savannah glanced quickly over at Thea, who smiled reassuringly. Everyone knew they were best friends, so of course they would be seated together.

Savannah didn't really listen until she heard Thea's name called out. She was shocked when she heard that Harry Morgan was Thea's seating partner—not her!

Before she knew what she was doing, Savannah exclaimed, "Mr. Chiochi, you can't do that!"

"What do you mean, 'I can't do that'?" Mr. Chiochi looked up, frowning at the interrup-

16

tion. "I should have known, Ms. Wheeler, that it would be you."

"She didn't quite mean it like that, Mr. Chiochi," Thea explained. "It's just that we promised our parents we would look out for each other, so we just have to sit together."

"That's the most ridiculous thing I've ever heard. If they wanted you to stay out of trouble, Ms. Tomaselli, they would have made sure you two were *not* together. I've decided to separate you two on the flight over just to avoid any possible problems."

"Ms. Martin, we did promise our parents we'd stick together," Savannah insisted, hoping her English teacher would be more understanding.

"I'm sure you two can still watch out for each other. You'll just be a few rows away—definitely within screaming distance."

"But—" Savannah protested, her panic of flying returning.

"There will be no changes. I've seated people the way I want, and I will not change my mind. Not another word, Ms. Wheeler." Mr. Chiochi turned away and continued down his list. "Mr. Cassorla and Ms. Lacey. Ms. Manley and Mr. Holzman. Mr. Edwards and Ms. Wheeler. That's it."

"Mr. Chiochi, if I can just explain," Savannah began, deciding she had to tell him about her fear of flying.

"Ms. Wheeler, I thought I said I didn't want to hear another word about this. It will be a difficult trip for both of us if this continues much

17

longer. The subject is closed." Mr. Chiochi turned and walked away, leaving Savannah with her mouth open.

"Come on, Savannah, can't you and Thea be apart for just a little while? I didn't think I would be so awful to sit next to," Greg teased.

"Oh, Greg, it's nothing against you. It'll be great to sit with you. It's just that . . . well, the moment Chiochi starts getting stubborn, I feel myself doing the same thing," Savannah quickly explained.

"Why does he pick on you so much?" Greg asked.

"I don't know. It's not like I've ever really done anything," Savannah lied, glad that she and Greg had never been in a class together before this year. "Excuse me, I'm just going to see if Thea is okay with this; it was really her mother we promised." Savannah rushed over to Thea, who was standing with some of their classmates.

"Thea, I have to talk to you," Savannah said, grabbing her friend's arm and pulling her away from the group. "What am I going to do? I'm going to freak out, and I can't do that in front of Greg."

"I don't know. Maybe you could tell him you're scared of flying," Thea advised.

"I can't. He thinks I'm so cool and together. Chiochi is so awful. He hates me!" Savannah wailed. "I don't know if I can ever get on that plane."

"Just keep your eyes closed and pretend it's me sitting next to you. If it gets really bad, we'll

18

tell Ms. Martin. Okay? You'll be fine." Savannah nodded mutely. "Now, go back to Greg; being with him should take your mind off flying. Hey, you know what, Savannah?" Thea asked after a moment. She had a dreamy look on her face that Savannah had never seen before.

"What?"

"Harry Morgan suddenly looks very cute to me. I don't know why I never noticed him before," Thea said, smiling and staring over at him.

"You didn't plan this, did you?" Savannah asked, suddenly suspicious.

"How can you say that? I would never desert you in your hour of need," Thea protested.

"I know. I'm sorry," Savannah apologized.

"We're boarding the plane now," Mr. Chiochi said sternly, suddenly appearing in front of the girls.

"Sorry," Savannah replied. She and Thea moved toward the other students who were already in line.

Slowly, the class boarded the plane and found their assigned seats. Savannah kept calm by staring at her feet on the way out to the plane. She tried to pretend she was walking down a school hallway as she stepped down the aisle of the plane. Greg graciously offered Savannah the window seat.

Savannah shook her head. "No, Greg, you can sit there."

"No, I insist," Greg said. "That way you can see the ground move away as the plane takes off, and all the houses and roads getting smaller and smaller. It's so neat."

Savannah felt her stomach lurch at Greg's description. She sat down next to the window and turned her body as far away from it as possible.

"Do you need help with your seat belt?" Greg asked as he watched Savannah nervously click her belt open and closed. Greg leaned over and carefully buckled it for her. Still leaning close to her, he lifted his head and looked up into her eyes. "Comfortable?" he whispered. She nodded blankly.

"Mr. Edwards, please focus on fastening your *own* seat belt," Mr. Chiochi warned. He was standing over them, tapping his pencil impatiently on his clipboard. Grinning, Greg moved back to his own seat and Mr. Chiochi walked on.

"He does seem always to come by at the worst times, doesn't he?" Greg laughed.

"Well, he'll have to sit down soon, too, and that will keep him away for at least a few minutes," Savannah answered, her heart beating from fear and excitement. There was no question in her mind now that Greg was interested in her. She couldn't wait to tell Thea. But she had to make sure she didn't do anything to jeopardize his feelings for her.

Suddenly, Savannah felt the plane moving. Instinctively, she grabbed Greg's arm. "What's going on?"

"It's just the plane, Savannah. It's taxiing

toward the runway. Are you all right?" Greg asked. "You look very pale."

Savannah couldn't answer. Her mouth was totally dry, and her mind had gone blank.

"Savannah, are you scared? Just nod if the answer is yes." Staring at him, she nodded. "Is this your first time on a plane?" She nodded again. "Poor Savannah, you're terrified. Why didn't you tell me? Here, grab onto my hand. Hey, your hands are freezing. Just take a deep breath and try to relax."

"It's—it's . . . I'm so embarrassed. I didn't want anyone to know. I feel so stupid." Savannah could feel the tears filling her eyes.

"Don't be embarrassed. I think it's the cutest thing. I didn't think you were afraid of anything. I like this part of you," Greg said.

"You do?" Savannah asked, gulping back some of her tears.

"Sure. Every guy likes to feel he can protect his favorite girl. And I can do a better job than Thea, so it's a good thing Chiochi put us together, isn't it?"

"Y-yes, I guess so," Savannah answered, suddenly thankful to Mr. Chiochi. She hadn't thought that Greg would be so kind and sweet.

"Guess what, Savannah?" Greg said a few minutes later, still holding her hands in his.

"What?" Savannah asked, swallowing hard to unclog her ears.

"We're flying," he answered, smiling.

"What!" Savannah turned around and faced the window and saw that they were already

21

skimming over the city of Boston. "You mean, that's it? That's what takeoff feels like?" When she grabbed Greg's shoulders, he nodded, laughing. "I did it! I survived takeoff! Oh, Greg, you're the greatest!" She undid her seat belt, then stood up and hugged him impulsively.

"Ms. Wheeler, sit down!" Mr. Chiochi ordered from his seat, five rows back. Greg pulled her back down and redid her belt.

"You're not allowed to unfasten your belt till that sign says so. Leave it to ol' Eagle Eyes to catch you," Greg teased.

"Greg, flying is great! I can't believe how scared I was. You were right—Boston looks so cool from up here. Thea will be so proud of me!" Savannah bubbled enthusiastically, searching for her home among the tiny buildings below.

"You mean you're not scared? You won't grab my arm anymore?" Greg half complained.

"Well, just because I'm not scared doesn't mean I don't want to hold hands," she teased him.

"Good," Greg answered. "You know something? I liked coming to your rescue."

"How are you doing?"

Savannah looked up, startled, to see Thea standing in the aisle.

"I thought we weren't allowed to leave our seats yet," Savannah said, puzzled.

"The seat-belt light just went off. I came by to see if you wanted to check out the ladies' room with me."

"Sure. Excuse me, Greg." Savannah hopped over Greg's legs and walked with Thea to the

22

back of the plane. Once there, Savannah hugged her best friend.

"You're obviously doing a lot better than I thought you would be," Thea grumbled. "I thought I would see you clutching the seat, your nails buried in the fabric."

"Thea, you wouldn't believe how sweet Greg was to me when he realized I was afraid of flying. He talked with me the whole time we took off, so I didn't even notice. But the best thing is that he liked that I was scared. He liked taking care of me. I was right all along—he is absolutely perfect. For once, Chiochi did something right!"

"Did you say he liked the fact that you were scared? That sounds kind of weird to me," Thea commented.

"I think he just meant he was glad I needed him, that's all." Savannah sighed. "He's the greatest. So how are you and Harry getting along?"

Thea hesitated for a moment before answering. "Okay. He's shy, but I think six hours should break the ice. I really like him."

"Great. Well, I'm going to head back to my seat now, before Chiochi finds something else to complain about. I wish we were sitting closer," Savannah complained.

"Me too," Thea agreed. "I guess we can meet back here again."

"Roger. Later, 'gator."

Savannah slowly made her way back to her seat. As she got closer, she thought about what she would do next to impress Greg. She giggled to herself as she imagined fainting into his arms. To her delight the plane hit a bit of turbulence as she got to her seat, and she let herself fall against Greg's shoulder.

"Oh, I'm sorry." She giggled lightly, and instead of moving away, she used the plane's motion to fall back against him. She looked up at his face through her lashes and saw that he was grinning.

"Ma'am, I'm afraid this seat is taken. I don't object, but I'm sure Chiochi is about to come by and scream," Greg said.

At the mention of Chiochi, Savannah sat up straight. She couldn't bear the thought of getting into trouble again.

"Now, where were we? Oh, yes, you were about to show me the sights down below," Savannah said, sighing happily as she stared into Greg's big brown eyes.

Chapter Three

"**S**avannah, wake up. We're in Stratford," Thea said, nudging her friend.

Savannah opened her eyes, immediately awake, and looked out the bus window. As the bus rolled up and down the narrow roads, heading toward the youth hostel, Savannah saw little pubs and stores, houses with thatched roofs, pastures with cows, stone fences—exactly the picturesque, quaint town she had imagined. "This is the most romantic place," she whispered. "Thea, we are *so* lucky!"

A whistle blast interrupted her reverie. Mr. Chiochi stood in the front of the bus holding his clipboard. "Listen up, people. Mr. Holzman and Mr. Cassorla, sit down." Savannah looked behind her and saw that they were standing, staring out the rear window of the bus. Greg was sitting nearby, eyes glued to the front of the bus. "In a little while, we will be at the Stratford Youth Hostel. When the bus has stopped, I want you to form a line and quietly exit. Ms. Martin and I will go in first and take care of the arrangements. While you are waiting, I don't want you running around. Stand quietly near the front entrance. Any questions? Good." Mr. Chiochi sat back down next to Ms. Martin at the front of the bus.

"Thea, how much do you want to bet that Chiochi is never separated from his clipboard or his whistle during this entire trip?" Savannah asked.

"It's a sucker's bet. You'll win too easily. I wish Ms. Martin was the only adult on this trip; she's so easygoing, and she trusts us," Thea complained.

"Thea, look!" Savannah interrupted, pointing out the window. As the bus climbed a hill, the two girls saw an old stone building set on a green lawn with trees in the distance. "Ooh, it's so beautiful. Is that the hostel?"

"I think so," Thea answered.

The bus pulled into the long driveway and parked. Under the precise direction of Mr. Chiochi, the students left the bus and waited on the lawn for the teachers to return.

"Hey, Savannah, I was thinking of you on the bus. I would have gladly sat next to you again and held your hand," Greg teased, walking over to her.

"She's not afraid of buses," Thea muttered under her breath.

"Isn't this place beautiful?" Savannah said quickly. "It's exactly like I hoped it would be. The birds are chirping; the air smells fresh. It all feels so English."

"It's perfect," Thea agreed with a smile.

"It's okay. But I'm not thrilled with the idea of sharing a room with three other guys or having to do chores," Greg told her, making a face.

Blushing, Savannah quickly agreed. "Oh, yes, it'll be a pain, but it's only for a short while. Anyway, it's so pretty."

"But we're so far from town."

Savannah kept quiet and just smiled brightly, nodding.

"Here comes Chiochi," Thea warned.

Chiochi whistled and everyone gathered around him. "All right, people, everything has been arranged," he announced, consulting his clipboard. "You will go to the bus one by one and get your bags. The hostel is split into two halves. The west half is for the boys, and the east half is for the girls."

The class interrupted him with loud groans and laughs.

"People, this is not funny. If I find anyone in the wrong area of the hostel, you will have to answer to me. There is a strict curfew here. The doors are locked at eleven P.M. The nights we see the plays, they will keep the doors open until we return—as a group. Girls, Ms. Martin is in your wing, and she has your room assignments. After you get your rooms, I suggest you all rest for a while. We will have dinner in town tonight."

The class, under the guidance of Mr. Chiochi, returned to the bus to get their bags and then headed to the designated areas.

The girls stopped when they reached Ms. Martin, who stood in the hallway.

"Isn't this building lovely?" she asked. "It used to be a country home, before it was turned into a hostel. The grounds are absolutely wonderful, and I'm sure we'll have time to explore them later on. Thea, Savannah, Elaine, and Emma, you're in this room. Danielle, Cameron, Madeleine, and Holly, you're across the hall. I have a room up the hallway, out of hearing distance from you. If I can hear you at night, then I know you're being too loud. Otherwise, you're on your own." Ms. Martin smiled at them. "It's two o'clock now. We're going to leave for dinner at six. I suggest you rest—it must be about eight in the morning at home—or sit outside. We'll meet down in the common room at five-thirty."

The girls went into their separate rooms, and Savannah and Thea claimed the same bunk bed. After unpacking some of her belongings and making her bed, Thea fell back across the bottom bunk. "I'm exhausted. I'm going to take a nap. What are you guys doing?"

"Definitely sleeping," Emma said. Elaine nodded in agreement.

"Come on, you guys," Savannah complained. "How can you sleep? This is our first afternoon in England. It's beautiful outside. Who wants to go exploring with me?"

"I will—tomorrow," Thea promised.

"What about you two?" Savannah asked, but it was obvious from Emma's and Elaine's prone positions that sleep was first on their minds. Savannah looked across the hallway and saw that the other four girls had already closed their door. "Well, I'm going outside. Maybe one of the guys will want to go."

"Except we're not allowed in their wing," Thea joked, yawning as she rolled over to face the wall. "Don't slam the door on your way out."

Savannah picked up her sweater, made a face at her three sleepy classmates, and walked quietly out of the room, down the wooden stairs. She peered around the common room and saw no one was there. She looked down the hallway that led toward the boys' rooms, but knew she would get caught if she even stepped over the threshold.

"I don't care if the entire hostel is asleep," she murmured to herself. "I'm going out. There's no way I'm going to waste one bit of my time here sleeping."

Putting on her sweater, Savannah slipped out the front door. She stared at the woods and then at the driveway and decided she was less likely to get lost if she stayed on a road. Savannah walked down the driveway, following the route that the bus had taken.

Humming softly to herself, Savannah walked on until she reached one of the stone fences that surrounded a cow pasture. Leaning on the fence, she just stood there, watching the cows, unaware of the time—reveling in the feeling that she was in England.

Humming a tune that her grandfather had

29

taught her when she was little, Savannah moved on, walking along the road toward town. Except for the paved road, it felt as if she were in England in the 1600s. Seeing no cars or people, Savannah could easily ignore the fact that she was wearing her black leggings and Reeboks. Instead she imagined herself in a long dress, walking to town to meet her true love.

"Except, silly, you've left your true love fast asleep in the hostel—probably snoring," Savannah reminded herself. Laughing out loud, she skipped the rest of the way until she reached town.

As she examined the townspeople, Savannah realized that although they didn't quite dress the way she and her friends did, they certainly didn't wear long dresses! Choosing to explore the small walks and alleys, Savannah stared at everything she passed until she came to a dead end—and realized she had no idea where she was.

Confused, she looked around the cul-de-sac and saw a small building that looked like a restaurant. There was a wooden sign above the door with the words "The Hart and Hounds" etched in it. She opened the heavy wooden door and entered the small pub.

A few men sat at the bar, talking to the bartender, who looked to be near her own age. Nervously, Savannah walked up to the bar.

"Excuse me," she said.

The conversation stopped and the three men stared at her. The boy behind the bar smiled. She directed her next comment to him.

"Um, I just got into town today and didn't pay attention to where I was going. And now I'm kind of lost. Could you tell me how to get back to the main road?"

"From the States, aren't you?" one of the men asked.

"Y-yes," Savannah answered, suddenly feeling very alone and very out of place.

"Staying up at the hostel?"

"Well, yes."

The man nodded. "Ginnie told me a group of students were coming in; she's one of the gals who help run the place," he explained.

"Da, you sound like you're cross-examining her. She'll think we're unfriendly here," the boy protested, still smiling at Savannah.

Savannah smiled back, hoping that would help. "Could you just tell me how to get back to the main road?"

"Do you need to get back to the hostel?" the boy asked. Savannah nodded. "Do you know how to do that?"

"No, not really," Savannah admitted. "I wasn't really paying attention. I was just so happy to be here."

"Philip, why don't you drive her back to the hostel?" the older man suggested. "It's a bit of a walk, especially on your first afternoon in England."

"Oh, no, sir. Thanks though," Savannah answered. "If you could just point out the way, maybe make me a little map, that would be great."

"Don't say another word. Philip will drive you. Or if you prefer, he'll hitch up the horse and wagon and take you there that way," the man continued.

"Horse and wagon?" Savannah repeated. "Wow, that sounds great." She clapped her hands and turned to Philip. "Is this okay with you?"

"If Da hadn't suggested it himself, I would have. It's definitely a long walk back. Would you like something to drink before we start?" Philip offered.

"Water would be great. I'm parched."

"Philip, give her some of your mum's cider," the second man suggested. "It's the best for miles around."

"Good idea, George."

Philip poured out a couple of glasses of cider. "What's your name?"

"Savannah," she answered after she took a big swallow of cider. "Mm, this is the best cider I've ever had."

Philip grinned. "I'll tell Ma, she'll be glad to hear it. I'm Philip Wescott. Come on out back with me while I hitch up the wagon."

"Savannah is a rather peculiar name," Philip commented as he led the horse to the wagon.

"My mother's from the South," Savannah explained. "Savannah's a city in Georgia."

"That's interesting. Here, I'll help you up," he offered after he finished hitching the horse to the wagon.

"No, I can do it myself," Savannah insisted as

32

she hoisted herself up on the wagon. Philip climbed up and smiled at her as he flicked the reins. The horses responded by moving slowly. "This here is Godiva. She's a sweet old thing, isn't she?"

"This is great. What do you use the wagon for? Do you have a farm?" Savannah asked.

Philip nodded. "We raise sheep. But we use this wagon for just about everything—carrying Mum's cider to the pub, shipping sheep, giving rides to pretty girls . . ."

Savannah gave him a swift look and then yawned loudly. "Sorry." She clapped her hand to her mouth. "I think the jet lag is finally hitting me." She yawned again and smiled apologetically.

"Don't worry about it. Just enjoy the ride," Philip instructed.

Savannah leaned back against the wooden seat. Fighting to keep her eyes open the whole trip took all her concentration.

"Savannah, we're here," Philip whispered as he stopped the wagon on the edge of the driveway. "Savannah, wake up."

"I'm awake." She opened her eyes and realized that she was leaning against the boy's shoulder. "Oh, I'm sorry."

"It's okay. I hate to tell you this, but I think you have a welcoming committee, of sorts."

Savannah sat up and looked toward the front of the hostel, where Mr. Chiochi was standing with several of her classmates.

"Uh-oh. What time is it?" she asked Philip.

"Twenty-five to six."

"I'm five minutes late. And I left the grounds—I don't know if I was allowed to do that."

"Would you like me to come up with you and help explain that you got lost?" Philip asked.

"No thanks." Savannah scrambled down from the seat. "I think I better handle this one myself. Thanks so much for the cider and the ride. Wish me luck." Savannah smiled briefly at Philip, her mind already on what she would say to Mr. Chiochi. She could feel his anger before she even neared the front door. Thea, Elaine, Greg, and Howard were standing with him.

Oh no, she thought, *what's Greg going to think when Chiochi yells at me—again?*

"I'm sorry I'm late, Mr. Chiochi," Savannah said as she stepped up the stairs.

"Where were you, Ms. Wheeler?" Mr. Chiochi's round face was red.

Glancing worriedly at Greg, Savannah began, "Well, everyone went to sleep as soon as we got here. I wasn't tired, so I—"

"I don't want to hear any excuses. Just tell me where you were."

"I'm trying to, Mr. Chiochi, if you'd let me." Savannah could see Thea shaking her head behind Mr. Chiochi. Taking a deep breath to calm down, Savannah continued, "I went to town and got lost."

"You what? Who brought you back here?"

"Oh, that was Philip. I met him in a bar." Savannah heard Thea groan and realized she had made a great tactical error. Out of the cor-

34

ner of her eye, she saw Greg's eyes widen. "I mean—you see, Mr. Chiochi—"

"Elaine, please get Ms. Martin," Mr. Chiochi interrupted, turning away from Savannah. Elaine quickly went inside and Savannah could hear her calling for the English teacher. "I don't want to hear another word until Ms. Martin comes out. Needless to say, I'm very disappointed in you, but not surprised, Ms. Wheeler."

"Oh, Savannah, you're back," Ms. Martin said mildly, coming out the door with Elaine. "Did you have a nice walk?"

"Ms. Martin, you do not realize the gravity of the situation. Ms. Wheeler walked to town and was just dropped off by some man in a wagon whom she picked up in a bar."

"That's not what I said, Mr. Chiochi! You didn't give me a chance to explain," Savannah protested, raising her voice. "Ms. Martin, that isn't what happened."

Ms. Martin looked at Mr. Chiochi's angry, worried face. "Mr. Chiochi, suppose we let Savannah tell us what happened before we make any assumptions."

"Th-thank you, Ms. Martin." Savannah glanced at Thea and Greg for support; Thea smiled encouragingly, but Greg's face looked closed off.

"I wasn't tired, so I decided to take a walk. I thought I might get lost if I went toward the woods, so I figured following the road was a safer bet. Well, I ended up walking to town by accident. And then I didn't stay on the main road; there were all these pretty little streets and alleyways that were so lovely. They were exactly how I imagined they would be and—"

"Go on with your story, Savannah," Ms. Martin prompted.

"Oh, sorry. Well, then I came to a dead end, and I realized I didn't know how to get back to the main road or the hostel, so I went into the only building that was open there, which turned out to be a pub. I only realized it was a pub when I went inside.

"Anyway, there were these three men and Philip—the boy who drove me back here. I told them I was lost and asked if they would tell me how to get back to the main road. That's when Philip's father offered to have Philip drive me back, which he did. Philip's father asked me if I wanted to be driven back in a car, but I said I'd prefer the wagon—oh, sorry, Ms. Martin." Savannah stopped rambling when she saw her teacher's warning look. "I fell asleep on the wagon; I guess I was more tired than I thought, especially after my walk.

"They were very nice and helpful, and they even gave me some homemade apple cider. I'm sorry if I did anything wrong," Savannah finished in a rush, looking earnestly at Ms. Martin.

"Well, Mr. Chiochi, I don't think anything too terrible happened. Savannah was only five minutes late, and we didn't specify that no one could leave the hostel without us," Ms. Martin concluded.

"But she was in a *bar*," Mr. Chiochi reminded her.

"No, she was in a pub. Pubs are different here from bars in the States. They're more of a family place, almost like a restaurant, and the gentlemen certainly sounded very polite and thoughtful. But Savannah, the next time you choose to leave the hostel, you should let someone know," Ms. Martin said.

"Yes, I will, Ms. Martin. Thank you," Savannah replied.

"Get your things, Ms. Wheeler. We're leaving for town in a few minutes." Mr. Chiochi gave Savannah one last stern look before he followed Ms. Martin into the hostel.

"Come on, Savannah, I'll go with you. I left something in our room," Thea said.

"Okay," Savannah said slowly, waiting for Greg to say something to her, but he only looked away.

It will be all right, Savannah told herself. *I'll make sure Greg sees that I just made a mistake, and I'll never do something like this again. This will be the last stupid thing I do the whole trip,* Savannah vowed to herself as she followed Thea into the hostel.

Chapter Four

"Savannah, don't be so upset. I'm sure Greg wasn't angry at you," Thea assured Savannah the next morning as they did their chore of sweeping up the rooms before breakfast.

"But he didn't sit next to me at dinner," Savannah argued.

"There wasn't any room, with all the girls wanting to know about the English boy you met!" Thea laughed. "I can't believe you don't remember what he looks like. From where I was standing, he looked pretty cute to me. And the accent must be great."

"Sorry, Thea. I can't remember. I think he had light brown hair, or maybe blond. I don't know. I wasn't really paying attention to him. I fell asleep, and the next thing I saw was Chiochi. That threw everything else out of my mind! Greg probably thinks I'm an idiot; no one else got into trouble on the first day," Savannah wailed.

"Why don't you see how he is today before

you get all upset? Brush that last pile of dust in here, and let's get to breakfast. I'm starved," Thea said.

The two girls quickly finished their job and rushed to the dining room, where most of the other students were already seated. Savannah looked around and saw Greg motioning to her—he had saved her a seat next to him. Smiling, Savannah turned questioningly to Thea.

"Savannah, I'm going to sit with Harry, okay?" Thea whispered.

"No problem. Let's compare notes afterward," Savannah suggested, grinning at her friend.

"Thanks for saving me a seat, Greg," Savannah said, sitting down after she picked up her bowl of oatmeal. "What was your chore this morning?"

"I have to wash the dishes after breakfast. So please lick your bowl clean—I hate washing," he said.

Savannah nodded, looking around. "Yeah, I would hate to wash up after this crew, too."

"You must have been really tired yesterday to pull such a stunt," Greg commented.

Savannah's spoon stopped halfway to her mouth. "What do you mean?"

"I mean it just didn't seem like you. Walking off to town and then coming back with some local guy in a wagon." Greg shook his head. "It doesn't take a brain to know that would really tick Chiochi off."

"I guess you're right," Savannah said slowly. "I was really tired, and if I'd been thinking

40

straight, I would have wandered around the grounds. But once I got lost, what else could I have done?"

"To come back in a wagon, Savannah—really," Greg went on.

"What was wrong with that?"

"I don't know. It was sort of embarrassing to stand there and watch you return by horse and wagon and then hear Chiochi reprimand you publicly. I mean," Greg hastily explained, "I was embarrassed for you."

"Th-thanks," Savannah mumbled, not sure if she felt grateful or not.

"You just didn't seem like the Savannah I know and like so much," Greg finished, smiling at her.

Not being able to resist, Savannah smiled back. "I see what you mean. I guess I wasn't thinking straight yesterday, or I would have been more responsible."

"I want to be truthful with you about how I feel. I think that's important, don't you?"

Savannah swallowed hard. "Yes, I do."

As she was about to lean toward him, she noticed a shadow falling over them. It was Mr. Chiochi.

"If you're about finished eating, I believe it is time for you to start washing up, Mr. Edwards. We have a lot to do today, and we want to get started as soon as possible."

"Yes, we're finished." Greg quickly scooped the last bit of oatmeal into his mouth, winked at Savannah, and walked out to the kitchen.

"I hope that we will not have any more difficulties, Ms. Wheeler. I do not enjoy having to watch you constantly, no matter what you may think," Mr. Chiochi said. "I would have hoped that after all these years, our relationship would become easier."

Savannah stared at Mr. Chiochi. He had never spoken to her as if she were an adult before. "I'll try my best, Mr. Chiochi. I don't mean to cause any problems; it just seems that the things I naturally do shouldn't be done. I'll try to keep my impulses in check."

"Fine. I th— Mr. Cassorla, what are you doing? That is no way to carry dishes." Mr. Chiochi abruptly left Savannah and went after Danny Cassorla, who was balancing the oatmeal bowls on his head.

Savannah grinned and finished her oatmeal quickly, then went to find Thea, who was sitting out behind the hostel.

"Thea, I've been looking all over for you," she said. "Why aren't you with Harry?"

"I don't want him to think I'm chasing him. Anyway, he had to go clean the boys' bathroom. We might have a silly job, but at least we don't have to do anything really gross."

"That's true. How are things with Harry, anyway?"

"Great," Thea answered, smiling. "He's so shy, but there's something special about him. . . . Anyway, I'm glad we're here. Isn't it beautiful?"

"Yes, it is. Can you imagine growing up here? The air is so clean and so soft." Savannah sighed as she sat down next to Thea on the bench.

"What happened with Greg the Great?"

"Thea, don't make fun of him."

"Sorry, I won't. But what happened?"

"He told me he thought we should always be truthful with each other. Do you know what that means? It means he thinks of us as a couple!" Savannah exclaimed.

"What did he say after the bit about being truthful?" Thea asked suspiciously.

"He said I wasn't acting like myself—'the Savannah he knows and likes,' " Savannah quoted smugly. "And that I must have been exhausted to go off the grounds to town and accept a ride from a stranger."

Thea turned to face her. "But Savannah, that's exactly like you. It just isn't like the Savannah you pretend to be around him."

"No, it's like the *old* Savannah. Starting today, I'm turning over a new leaf, as they say. Greg was right. I wasn't acting mature yesterday, and I need to grow up. Even Mr. Chiochi spoke to me like I was an adult today. Oh, Thea, I like Greg so much. When he smiles at me or even looks at me, I melt. I'll be any way he wants me to be," Savannah said fervently.

"You mean no more imagining wild stories, no more peeking behind closed doors, no more dancing in the streets?" Thea looked disappointed.

"Not if it's not mature behavior. Besides, why do I need to imagine anything if I have Greg by my side?"

"By your side? I didn't want to say anything,

but I didn't like the way he acted after you came back from town yesterday. He wouldn't look at you, and he didn't think what you did was interesting or funny. How can you fall for someone who doesn't have your sense of humor—or any sense of humor?"

"Thea, if you don't have anything nice to say about Greg, then don't say anything at all," Savannah insisted, raising her voice.

The two friends sat silently on the bench, not looking at each other. Savannah played with the hem of her oversize shirt. "I'm sorry I yelled at you, Thea," she said a moment later.

"I'm sorry too. I won't say anything bad about Greg again, but—"

"Thea!" Savannah warned.

"Sorry." Thea shrugged, grinning. "If you turn mature or whatever you want to call it, don't expect me to be very happy. Life just won't be as much fun."

"Oh, Thea, of course it will," Savannah promised, putting her arm around her friend's shoulders. "It will be different from what we're used to, and that should be fun—I hope."

"Oh, no. There's Chiochi's whistle again." Thea sighed.

"You know, they should make people get a license for those things," Savannah complained.

"Was that a mature thing to say, Ms. Wheeler?" Thea teased as the two girls rose to go back inside the hostel.

At the sound of Mr. Chiochi's whistle, the entire class gathered in the common room of the hostel, where Mr. Chiochi instructed everyone to be ready in ten minutes to leave for town.

Savannah and Thea rushed to their room to get their cameras and knapsacks.

"At last, Thea, we're on our way. What's our first stop, do you know?" Savannah asked, putting on her hat and making sure she had paper, pens, and enough money in her knapsack.

"Ann Hathaway's house," Thea told her as she brushed her hair back into a ponytail.

"Oh, I can't wait!" Savannah cried.

"Have you seen my sweater?" Elaine asked, appearing in the doorway. "Savannah, you're not wearing that hat, are you?"

"What's wrong with it?" Savannah asked, touching her favorite hat tentatively.

"I don't know; it just looks silly. Anyway, hurry up. We're supposed to be at the bus in a minute." Elaine dashed out of the room.

Savannah turned to Thea. "Does it really look funny?"

"Not to me. I love that hat," Thea answered.

"Yeah, but if Elaine thought it looked silly, so will Greg." She tore the hat off her head and threw it on the bed.

"I thought you loved that hat!"

"Not anymore. And I don't want to hear anything else about it," Savannah said crossly, grabbing her knapsack and leaving the room.

She and Thea joined the other students and boarded the bus. Savannah felt better when she and Thea sat down across the aisle from

45

Greg, who smiled warmly at her. She turned to look out the window as the bus passed the same pasture she had stopped at the afternoon before. She was so happy to finally be in England. She thought about how much fun it would have been if she and her grandfather had been able to travel together. Even though he had passed away five years ago, she still missed him intensely.

"Hey, Savannah, do you see the pub where you were last night?" Thea asked, interrupting Savannah's thoughts.

"No, I doubt I'd even recognize the street I walked down," Savannah answered. The bus stopped across the street from a small, thatched-roof building with a lovely little garden in front.

"Listen up, everyone. Our first stop is Ann Hathaway's house. Once you get outside, line up at the front entrance and wait for further instructions," Mr. Chiochi answered.

"Why does he treat us like we're five years old?" Savannah mumbled.

"Doesn't he realize you're a mature woman of thirty-five?"

"Thea!" Savannah warned as the two girls laughed and left the bus. Outside, as Savannah glanced around at the small street, the houses, and the beautiful gardens surrounding it, she felt a surge of happiness.

"You don't want a fly to land there, do you?" Greg said, coming up beside her.

Savannah looked at him, confused. "What?"

"Your mouth—it was open."

46

"Oh, sorry. I was just impressed by how pretty everything is," Savannah answered, quickly regaining her composure.

"Chiochi's signaling us to enter through the portals of this quaint house," Greg informed her. He rolled his eyes.

"You don't like it?" Savannah asked.

"It's okay. But I prefer the cities to places like this, don't you?" Greg asked as they walked down the path toward the front door.

"Well, yes, but I think it's interesting to see how people in small towns lived," Savannah lied. She much preferred the country to the city. As they entered the house, Savannah let Greg move ahead while she waited for Thea.

The class had their own special tour guide, Ms. Henry, who explained that Ann Hathaway had been William Shakespeare's wife and gave a brief history of their life together. Then she pointed out the special features and possessions in the room.

The class moved on to the next room, leaving Savannah and Thea behind. The two girls just stared at the antiques.

"Thea, can you believe all this neat old stuff?" Savannah asked.

Thea moved toward her friend, who was staring longingly at a small, delicate-looking chair in the corner.

"I just want to sit down for a second here. I have to know what it feels like. . . ." Savannah glanced around, making sure that they were completely alone in the room, and sat down. Her

47

eyes closed, she smiled and wiggled more comfortably on the chair.

"Okay, Savannah, get off. You've had your feel of history," Thea whispered.

"Miss Wheeler!"

"Mr. Chiochi!" Savannah cried, jumping off the seat. At the sound of his voice, Ms. Henry, Ms. Martin, and some of the other students returned to the room.

"What were you doing on that chair?" Mr. Chiochi demanded, striding toward her.

"S-sitting." Savannah gulped. Greg was standing right behind Ms. Martin.

"Perhaps you didn't realize that this is a museum," Ms. Henry suggested.

"I'm really sorry, but . . . well, it's hard to explain—I just had to know what it felt like to sit there. All I could imagine was Ann Hathaway sitting in that chair and—"

"That's enough, Ms. Wheeler. I think you've done enough damage. And you, Ms. Tomaselli."

"Don't blame Thea. She didn't do anything!" Savannah insisted angrily. "I'm the only one who sat on the chair!"

Restraining a smile, Ms. Martin said, "Well, I'm glad to hear that. Perhaps, Savannah, in the future you can control some of your enthusiasm when it involves other people's property—especially priceless historical objects."

"Yes, Ms. Martin. I am sorry. Sometimes I just don't always think before I act."

"You certainly do not," Mr. Chiochi agreed. "I'm tempted to send you back to the hostel, but I think it will be enough if you wait for us outside in the garden. Just don't touch anything, don't pull out any of the flowers, don't do any weeding."

"I get the point," Savannah muttered. "I will—I mean, I won't," Savannah said miserably as she saw Greg look at her, turn away, and leave the room. "Please forgive me, Ms. Henry, I didn't mean to do any harm. You just don't know how it feels to be so close to all this and not touch it or try to live it. If only I could tell you what I was imagining—"

"Enough, Ms. Wheeler. Your imagination has led you into trouble your whole life," Mr. Chiochi said dryly.

"There hasn't been all that much damage, Mr. Chiochi," Ms. Henry quickly said. She turned to Savannah. "I can well imagine what you were feeling. My love of history is what made me take this job, but even I am not allowed to sit on the chairs."

"Savannah, wait for us in the garden," Ms. Martin advised. "It's time for us to go on with the tour."

"I'll go with her, Ms. Martin," Thea volunteered.

"Thea, that's not necessary," Savannah protested. "Don't miss out on anything because of me."

"I don't mind. We'll be out back," Thea said.

"I'm sorry, Thea," Savannah said as the two girls wandered along the stone path in the old-fashioned herb gardens. "You didn't need to miss the rest of the tour."

49

"I prefer being outside than in there," Thea insisted. "Here, smell this, isn't it great?" Thea said, rubbing a sprig of lavender between her fingers.

"Umm, that's great. Thanks for sticking by me; you don't know how much I appreciate that. And I thought I was all finished doing stupid things." Savannah sighed.

"Well, it's not easy to change a lifelong habit, you know."

"Thea!" Savannah laughed. "It's so typical of me. I vowed I would be mature, and what do I do when the first temptation comes my way? I give in to it. And Greg saw Chiochi yelling at me again. I'm so embarrassed! If I keep doing these things, he's not going to want to be with me anymore."

"But, Savannah, why change yourself for a guy who doesn't approve of the real you?" Thea asked, sitting down on a white stone bench in the bright sunlight.

"But getting into trouble isn't the real me. It's the old me, the young me, and I'm not going to do it anymore," Savannah declared.

"It's not the getting into trouble part—it's your imagination and your enthusiasm that he doesn't seem to like. And those are some of your best qualities!" Thea argued.

"Well, other people are imaginative, and they don't make fools of themselves."

Thea chuckled. "Not to discourage you, but I don't think it's possible for you *not* to let yourself go. Besides, as I said before, I'd miss that part of you. Remember when we climbed to the top of Mr. Peterson's roof to look in their skylight because you were sure he had killed Mrs. Peterson?"

Savannah laughed. "That was pretty awful. But I was so sure! Although I'm glad it wasn't true."

"And what about the time when you wanted to run away with the circus?" Thea turned her face to the sun, her eyes closed. "But my favorite is the time we made that haunted house in your basement."

"That was great," Savannah agreed. "Of course, locking Leanne Saunders down there did cause some problems. Not getting my mother's permission was another big goof, but at least we raised money for a good cause. We should host another haunted-house party when we get home —we would be so much better at it now."

"We can't. You've decided never to do anything immature again," Thea reminded her.

"Well, maybe every once in a while I can slip back into the crazy days of my youth."

The two girls looked at each other and laughed.

Chapter Five

Savannah and Thea sat on the bench talking until the class finished their tour and came out to see the garden. Harry walked directly to where the girls were sitting.

"Hi, I heard what happened," he said. "Too bad you were caught. I was tempted to try out the bed in the other room, but Chiochi kept a watchful eye on all of us."

"Thanks, Harry," Savannah replied. "What are we doing next?"

"Hanging out in the garden a bit and then walking to a pub—isn't that great? Ms. Martin has one picked out. She says it's the best place in town to eat lunch," Harry informed them.

"Well, I've seen the garden, but maybe you want to show Harry some of the best parts, Thea," Savannah suggested.

"Great idea," Harry agreed. Thea shot Savannah an exasperated—but happy—look as she and Harry left to stroll around the garden.

Sitting alone on the bench, Savannah felt the

beauty of the garden overwhelm her. Impulsively, she stood up and exclaimed, " 'This bud of love, by summer's ripening breath, may prove a beauteous flow'r when next we meet.' "

"Talking to yourself now! Don't let Chiochi catch you," Greg teased. He had sneaked up behind her and was sitting on the bench.

"G-Greg," Savannah stuttered. "Greg, I'm—"

"Savannah, why—" They both started at once. "You go first."

"No, you."

Greg took a deep breath. "Why did you do it? You knew it was wrong. I mean, what's come over you? Since we've been here, you've been acting so strangely. It's like you just don't think about what you're doing."

"You sound a lot like Chiochi right now," Savannah said, her temper flaring.

"Well, I happen to agree with him. Any eight-year-old kid knows you're not supposed to touch things in a place like that."

Savannah felt stricken by the truth of his statement, and her anger subsided. "I know," she said contritely. "I just had to know what it felt like to sit on that chair. The impulse overcame me. Maybe it's jet lag. I'm still not thinking clearly."

"I felt awful, hearing Chiochi yell at you in front of everyone," Greg confessed.

"Thanks. I thought you were angry at me."

"I was—and embarrassed. It must be sort of obvious that we're a couple, and having my girlfriend publicly humiliated reflects on me."

54

"I see. I'm sorry I embarrassed you," Savannah said stiffly. "Can we stop talking about this now?"

"Sure." Greg shrugged. He looked at his watch and stood up. "We're supposed to meet in front of the house in a couple minutes to walk to lunch. Let's go." He took her hand, and together they walked toward the other students.

Thea was standing with Harry, and she shot Savannah a questioning look. Savannah just smiled and nodded slightly toward her hand in Greg's. Thea smiled back, giving her a thumbs-up.

The class walked as a group on the main road, then turned down a small lane that forked into a dead end. At the end of the lane was a charming pub.

Stepping into the pub, Savannah saw that they were the last ones to enter and there were only two seats left—at two different tables.

"I guess I'll see you after lunch," Greg whispered, squeezing her hand. Savannah nodded and sat down at a table with Thea, Elaine, and Emma.

"Savannah, what do you want? One of us from each table is supposed to go up and order," Elaine said.

"I'll have the plowman's lunch," Savannah said.

"I'm getting a shepherd's pie; let's split them," Thea suggested. Savannah nodded, and Elaine went up to the bar to give their order.

"I ordered a Scotch egg. I hope it's good," Emma said when Elaine sat back down.

"It's probably an egg wrapped in a little plaid outfit," Savannah teased her.

"Did everyone want water?" a familiar male voice asked.

"That sounds great," Savannah said, looking up.

"Hi, Savannah." It was Philip.

Savannah burst out laughing. "No wonder this place looks so familiar. I was here yesterday! I'm such an idiot!" she said, hitting herself lightly on the forehead. "Thanks for the ride home yesterday, Philip."

"It was no problem. Did you get into trouble?" he asked as he placed the glasses of water on the table.

Savannah looked at the other girls at the table before answering. "No more than usual and less than today." She felt Emma kick her under the table. "Oh, Philip, these are my friends, Emma, Thea, and Elaine. This is Philip, whose father owns this pub and who gave me a ride home yesterday."

"Hi. How do you like Stratford?" Philip asked.

"It's great," Emma said. The other girls nodded.

"I'll see you a little later. I have to give the rest of the tables their water, too. You Americans drink so much water!"

As soon as he left, the three girls turned to Savannah.

"Savannah, you never said he was so cute!" Emma whispered.

Savannah shrugged. "I didn't notice."

"How could you not notice those incredible blue eyes or that grin?" Thea demanded.

56

"And that accent!" Elaine pretended to swoon.

"Of course he has an accent! You guys are being so silly," Savannah scolded.

"*Us* silly? You're blind not to see the way he was looking at you," Thea said.

"Of course he was looking at me! He knows me. He was just being friendly," Savannah argued.

"Come on, Savannah. He wasn't just looking at you. He was *looking* at you." Emma giggled. "You know what I mean."

"Who has the plowman's lunch?" Philip suddenly appeared at their table. The three girls guiltily looked at him and then giggled.

"I do. Thank you," Savannah answered.

"Shepherd's pie?" He placed that in front of Thea. "Who wanted the Scotch egg?" Emma raised her hand slightly and looked with dismay at the breaded egg. "Do you want something else? We could heat you up a shepherd's pie quickly," Philip offered.

"Yes, please. This just doesn't do it for me," Emma admitted, smiling at Philip.

"And another plowman's lunch." Philip placed the last lunch in front of Elaine. "Savannah, I don't know what your schedule is, but would you like an untouristy tour of Stratford? I'd be glad to show you around."

Savannah looked at the other girls and then glanced over at Greg's table, where he was busy talking to the guys. All of a sudden, Greg seemed to be purposely ignoring her. He acted more interested in the guys than in her. And she hadn't appreciated the way he'd spoken to her that morning, either.

Defiantly she raised her chin. "We have a free day tomorrow. If you can do it then, I'd love to go."

"Great. I'll meet you at the hostel around ten. I'll come back with your shepherd's pie shortly," Philip told Emma.

"Don't say a word, any of you," Savannah said fiercely once he had gone. "He is cute, but he's just being nice to me. Just like you think it's cool that he's English with his accent and all, he probably thinks it'll be neat to hang out with an American."

"Especially a pretty American girl," Thea teased.

"I'm not interested in him. But I do think it'll be great to see Stratford with someone who lives here," Savannah said.

"What do you think Greg will say?" Emma asked.

"What do you mean?"

"Savannah, it's obvious to all of us that Greg's interested in you. Or more than interested in you. Didn't you notice him staring over here when Philip was talking with you?" Thea asked.

"No. Was he?" Savannah looked over at Greg's table and saw him talking animatedly with Howard and Danny. "He doesn't seem to be very interested in me now."

"Of course not. You're only with girls right now," Elaine explained.

"Then I'm glad I accepted Philip's offer," Savannah declared, trying not to think of Greg's probable reaction. "It shouldn't make a difference if I'm with friends who are girls or guys!"

"I don't think that's how Greg would see it. But going out with Philip might make him notice you even more. I think it's a good ploy," Elaine said.

"I'm not going out with Philip as a ploy, Elaine."

"Just don't do it more than once or twice while you're here," Elaine advised, ignoring Savannah's replies. "Greg is definitely the best guy in our grade."

"Definitely the best-looking. And very cool," Emma agreed. "You two look great together."

"I don't know. Personally, I think Harry's the best guy in our grade," Thea said softly.

"You do?" Emma squealed.

"Harry's nice, Thea, but Greg is just all-around perfect," Elaine said between bites of her shepherd's pie.

Savannah rolled her eyes. "All-around perfect, Elaine? You make it sound like this is the Olympics."

"Well, I still think Harry has it over every single boy in this pub, and that includes Greg and Philip," Thea stated firmly.

"And that's what's called true love, folks," Emma concluded.

Chapter Six

"I'm so exhausted," Cameron complained, sitting on the floor and wrapping her arms around her legs.

"It's probably because of the time difference," Holly answered. "This is a great fire, guys."

After a full day of sight-seeing, everyone had collapsed in the main room in the hostel. Greg and Howard had made a fire in the fireplace, and now most of the class was gathered around the blaze.

"Tomorrow night is the play," Savannah said enthusiastically. "I can't wait to see how they interpret *Romeo and Juliet*."

"Hey, Savannah, do you still have your monologues memorized?" Danny teased.

"Of course I do. They're just so beautiful, how could I forget them?" Savannah replied.

"Why don't you recite one?" Cameron asked.

"Oh, no. I couldn't," Savannah protested, laughing.

61

"Come on, Savannah," Harry encouraged her. "You know you want to, and you're so dramatic."

"You were the best one in class," Holly told her as a number of the others nodded in agreement.

Standing up, Savannah looked at the faces of her smiling friends and saw that they wanted her to recite. She glanced at Greg, whose face didn't reveal anything. Slowly, she sat back down and shook her head. "No, I'd feel silly. I prefer to see how the actress says them tomorrow night," she answered quietly. She was rewarded by a smile from Greg, but she saw Thea frowning from her spot in the corner. Not sure what to do, Savannah quickly got up and walked out of the room and outside.

Shivering in the slight breeze, Savannah walked to the back of the hostel and sat on the stone bench. Gazing up at the bright stars shining in the black sky, Savannah began to recite.

"Come, gentle night," she began. "Come, loving, black-brow'd night, give me my Romeo, and, when I shall die, take him and cut him out in little stars . . ."

"I hope you don't plan to cut *me* out in little stars," Greg said, coming up behind her.

"Greg!" Savannah whirled around, relieved that the night hid her blushing face.

"You're so cute when you're reciting."

"Cute?"

"Yeah, cute. Go on," Greg urged, sitting on the stone bench. "For a moment, I thought you

62

were going to do a monologue in front of everyone back there."

"And if I were?"

"Do you really think they wanted you to? They were just teasing, and you were about to believe them."

Savannah felt tears in her eyes and hoped Greg couldn't see them in the dark night. "I didn't think they were teasing me. Why would they do something like that?" she asked, turning back to the stars.

"I don't think they meant to be nasty, but, really, would you want to hear someone quoting Shakespeare?"

Savannah didn't answer and continued staring at the stars.

"You're shivering. I brought you a jacket," Greg said, placing one of his jackets around her shoulders.

"Thanks. I was kind of cold."

"Why did you leave?" Greg asked.

"I wanted to see what the stars look like here," she lied.

He laughed. "Stars look the same everywhere. You're so funny."

"Funny?" Savannah repeated. She moved back a few inches, away from Greg.

"Different, I mean. Hey, tomorrow's our free day, and I wanted to ask if we could do something together. How about it?"

Savannah turned back to him. "I would really love to, but I already agreed to spend my day with Philip."

Greg frowned. "Who's Philip?"

"The boy who brought me back here yesterday. We were in his father's pub today, and he was serving everyone. Remember?" Savannah asked.

"I didn't notice him," Greg said abruptly, turning away from her.

"Really?" Savannah remembered how the other girls had said that Greg was watching her while Philip was at their table. "Not even when he served your table?" she asked.

"Why are you spending the whole day with him?" Greg suddenly demanded.

"He asked me, and I didn't have any plans at that time. I thought it would be neat to see Stratford with someone who actually lives here," Savannah replied.

Greg folded his arms across his chest. "Yeah, right."

"Greg, he's just giving me a tour. It's not a date." Savannah paused, trying to imagine how Elaine would handle the situation. She seemed to know all the rules of dating. "Why? Are you jealous?"

"Of course not," Greg said.

"Good, because there's nothing to be jealous of. If I had known you wanted to spend time together, I would have picked you over him in a second."

"Can't you just tell him no now?"

"No. That wouldn't be right. Besides, I do want to see Stratford with him. I don't know when I'll get another chance to see England with someone who lives here. It means so much to me," Savannah explained. "And you and I have the next two weeks together—and more."

"You're a strange one, Savannah Wheeler," Greg said softly, moving closer to her. "I don't know who you are most of the time anymore. You're not the same girl I knew back in the States. I think England has bewitched you."

"You're not still angry that I'm going around with Philip tomorrow, are you?" Savannah said, her face inches from his.

"No, I just wish it were me." Greg leaned forward and softly kissed her. Savannah shivered, and he moved closer and put his arms around her and kissed her again. "I've been wanting to do this for ages."

Savannah opened her eyes briefly and saw Greg's lashes hiding his eyes, the stars bright behind his head. Sighing happily, she closed her eyes and kissed him back.

Their heads separated, and they smiled at each other.

"Uh-er, excuse me," Danny stammered. "But it's lights out soon, and Chiochi's on the prowl."

"Thanks for the warning, Dan," Greg said, grinning. "We'll be right in."

Danny nodded and quickly left them alone again.

"Pretty amazing that Chiochi didn't catch us," Savannah joked.

"Well, I'm glad we snuck in a few kisses without him around," Greg said, getting up. "We'd better go inside."

Savannah nodded, and hand in hand, they walked to the front door. Before they went in, Greg turned to her and kissed her one last time.

"Think of me tomorrow. And remember, you belong to me," he whispered. He let her go and opened the door.

Savannah touched her lips, still feeling the warmth of Greg's kiss. Caught between the softness of his kiss and the determination of his words, Savannah's heart beat rapidly.

You belong to me echoed in Savannah's ears. She thought she would have loved to hear someone say that to her, but instead she felt uneasy. She didn't want to belong to Greg; she wanted to be with him.

Doesn't he know the difference? Savannah thought to herself as she followed Greg into the well-lit hallway.

Chapter Seven

"Hi, Philip!" Savannah said when she saw Philip walking to the drive toward the hostel.

"Ready to see Stratford as never before?" Philip called out, grinning.

"Definitely," Savannah replied, jumping down the stone steps.

"I thought we would walk. Later on I can drive you back if we get really tired."

"Great. Let's go." Companionably they walked down the drive and along the road toward town. Philip pointed to the pasture where Savannah had watched the cows a few days ago.

"Let's cut across. It's a shortcut to town," Philip said. They both climbed over the fence and began the walk across the pasture. "Mind where you step—the cows definitely like to leave souvenirs everywhere."

"I'm glad you warned me," Savannah said, laughing.

"How long are you staying in Stratford?"

"For the next four days, and then we go to

London for four days, and then back to Boston," Savannah answered as she breathed in the clear, cool air. "It's beautiful here."

"Isn't it?"

"Oh, look, cows! English cows!" Savannah cried, clapping her hands together.

"That's their best cow." Philip pointed to a large black cow that stood away from the others. "Clara wins lots of prizes at the fairs. You want to pat her?" Philip asked. Savannah nodded enthusiastically.

Slowly, Philip walked to Clara and scratched her behind the ears. He then gestured to Savannah to imitate him. She scratched Clara's wide head and was rewarded by a low mooing.

"She likes you." Philip laughed. "You have a way with animals."

"It's great to learn my hidden talents," Savannah joked.

She was silent for a moment, enjoying the sunshine and the feel of the cow's silky hair beneath her fingers.

"Why aren't you in school?" Savannah asked.

"Spring break. We have two weeks off. Besides, who could be in school on such a beautiful day?" Philip asked, spreading his arms wide.

Savannah agreed wholeheartedly—the sun was shining, the sky was a beautiful shade of blue, and more birds were singing than she had heard in a long time. *And*, she thought to herself, *I am with this incredibly great guy. What a perfect day!*

"Let's keep going," Philip said.

" 'Bye, Clara." Savannah gave the cow a final scratch and followed Philip down a slight hill. "This is exactly the kind of English spring day I've always imagined."

"You're a great one for imagining," Philip said, with obvious admiration in his voice.

"I plan to be a writer," Savannah confessed. "At first I thought I only wanted to be a playwright, but now I know I need to try different types of writing and see what I'm best suited for."

"Do you write now?" Philip asked.

"Uh-huh. I write short stories. I've always wanted to write about England, but I only knew about it secondhand—and in my imagination," she explained.

"If we go over this fence and then down that path, we'll be in town," Philip directed. They were silent as they scrambled the fence and started on the path. "Why are you so in love with England?"

Savannah glanced at Philip, then looked down, not knowing whether to trust him with her memories of her grandfather.

"You don't have to tell me if you don't want to," he offered quietly.

At the sound of his voice, she stole a glance at him and saw concern in his face. She realized immediately that her grandfather would have liked Philip. "No, I can tell you. I can't believe I still get upset." She took a deep breath.

"My grandfather was English and left England when he was ten, but he used to tell me stories

69

about his childhood all the time. He grew up in the country, and he would describe everything, and I would imagine what it all looked like. He died when I was twelve, but I still miss him so much. . . .

"He was a great storyteller and made England so real and magical to me. It's only when I got older that I realized how hard life must have been for him and his family." Savannah smiled. "He went to London once, and he had some great stories about that trip. But my favorites are the ones about him and his brothers. My grandfather taught me how to read, too, so it's through him, I guess, that I get my love of writing.

"Anyway," Savannah continued in a rush, "my dream has always been to come to England. Being here makes me feel both wonderfully happy and so sad—because I wish he were here with me."

"I bet he is here with you," Philip said softly. "Your talking about him made him come alive for me."

"Thanks, Philip. That's exactly how I feel when I talk about him. That he's right here with me." Savannah suddenly felt very close to this boy she barely knew. She turned away so he couldn't see the sudden blush on her face.

"And here's town," Philip said, pointing. "I thought we could go to the market—from what I understand, people shop very differently here from what they do in the States. Afterward we can have lunch at my house and then a special treat."

"What?"

"I can't tell you—it's a surprise," Philip said, grinning.

Over the next few hours, they walked along some of the streets that Savannah had explored two days earlier. Only now, with Philip's explanations, the town made sense to her and places started to look familiar.

Everyone seemed to know Philip, and the different stall and store owners gave Savannah different foods to try once they discovered she was from the United States and a friend of Philip's.

"Philip, it's your friend from your pub!" Savannah said as they arrived at the fresh produce stall.

"George, you remember Savannah."

"Aye, the lass who was lost. You seem to have found your way today," George joked. "Can I interest you in some fruit?"

"No thanks, George. I'm just showing Savannah the way we shop. We're heading toward home to get some lunch," Philip explained.

"Great to see you again, George," Savannah said before she and Philip started walking to his house.

"Come visit again and we'll play a game of darts!" George called after them.

"That would be great, Philip!" Savannah exclaimed. "Playing darts in an English pub."

"Another dream come true?" Philip teased.

Savannah looked at him sharply and realized that although he was teasing her, he understood her excitement. She smiled and nodded. "I don't drink beer, but maybe I could have some of your mother's cider in a mug while I play." Savannah sighed mournfully. "Unfortunately, I can't imagine Chiochi allowing me to do *any* of this."

"Is Chiochi the man who was waiting for you?" Philip asked.

"Yes, he's in charge of our school trip. Philip, is *this* your house?" Savannah stopped suddenly as they stood before a small white house set off the road. It had a garden filled with crocuses, tulips, and daffodils. A trellis leading to the front door was covered with green vines.

"Isn't it pretty? It's called Heart's Ease. My grammy named it years ago when she first lived here."

"Ooh," Savannah sighed rapturously. "Even your home has a great name. It's perfect."

"Come inside," Philip offered eagerly.

The first room Savannah saw was the living room; there was a huge fireplace, and the furniture was more comfortable and homey than modern. The chairs were deeply cushioned, and homespun rugs covered the wooden floors. Sunlight poured through the lace-curtained windows, creating sparkling designs on the white walls.

"Up those wooden stairs are the bedrooms, and down this hallway is the kitchen," Philip explained, leading Savannah into the kitchen, which had a fireplace as well as modern appliances. The big kitchen table was wooden, and it was placed so that the early afternoon sun fell on it directly.

Looking out the window, Savannah saw a large expanse of green. Part of the backyard was a vegetable garden, another plot of land was devoted to flowers, and the rest just extended as far as she could see until her eyes stopped at a pond. "You have a pond?" she asked.

Philip nodded. "In the summers it's great. It's a little early yet. My ma left us some stew and one of her incredible pies for dessert. Sound good to you?"

"Perfect."

They ate hungrily in silence and Savannah spent most of her time gazing out the window. She pictured herself in a simple blue linen dress and a straw hat, picking strawberries while her grandfather and Philip played horseshoes. Just as she heard the clink of the horseshoe hitting the stake, she remembered with a start where she was. Embarrassed, she glanced at Philip, who simply smiled at her.

Toward the end of dessert, Savannah finally tore her eyes away from the gardens. "I was wondering if this is how my grandfather's home was," she told Philip. "I mean he probably walked in the same kind of pasture we did, and he probably knew all the shopkeepers like you do."

"Too bad Grammy is away. You two would

really like each other. Maybe you'll see her the next time you come to visit."

"I hope there will be a next time," Savannah said, her eyes shining. "Forget about hope—I'll make sure there's a next time."

"I'm sure you will," Philip said approvingly. "You finished?"

"Is it time for my surprise?" Savannah asked. Philip nodded. "This whole day so far has been a wonderful surprise!" Savannah leapt up from her chair, knocking it over. "Oh, gosh, I'm sorry . . ."

"It's no big deal," Philip said as they put everything away. "I'll do the dishes later. Let's go."

"Where are we going?" Savannah asked as they stood on the road outside of Philip's house.

"I can't tell you. But we are going as far as that road down there and then turning left."

"Race you to the road!" Savannah yelled, and started to run. Surprised, Philip didn't begin running for a few seconds, and Savannah was able to stay ahead. But in the last few yards, he passed her and won.

"You're fast," Philip said once they had stopped.

"I know," Savannah laughed, her cheeks pink from the exertion. "Hardly anyone beats me. I'm impressed."

"So am I! We'll have to try this again—without a head start for you. Come on." Philip grabbed her hand, and together they ran at a comfortable speed down the road before slowing to a walk. They walked back through the town, then

Philip led her along the banks of the river until they came to a little dock. He pointed to a small blue boat, which was tied to the dock. "I thought you might enjoy an historical ride on the Avon."

"Philip, this is the absolute best. Oh, thank you!" Savannah exclaimed, throwing her arms around him.

Philip hugged her back lightly. "Here, you get in and I'll push off."

Savannah stepped into the boat, and Philip tossed her the rope before he scrambled in.

Savannah sat facing the stern, her fingers trailing in the water while Philip rowed. "This is the life." She sighed. "Thank you."

"My pleasure," Philip responded.

"Anytime you want to switch, tell me."

"Don't tell me you're on the crew team too!"

"No," Savannah laughed. "My dad and I do a lot of rowing and sailing. However, I *am* perfectly content to sit here and pretend. . . ."

"Pretend what?"

"Well, don't laugh. But if I was stretched out, I could be dead Elaine on her barge from the King Arthur stories. I think I'd rather be alive Savannah today, though. So what do you want to be when you grow up?"

"An architect," Philip answered. "Well, not exactly. I want to restore old buildings and monuments as well as create some of my own. But I mainly want to fix all the ones that have been destroyed by the war or by time. I'm fascinated by old places and history; I don't think people should lose the physical remnants of their history."

"That's so neat, Philip," Savannah said, sitting up. Suddenly the sun came through the trees and lit up Philip's face. His sky blue eyes sparkled, and the gold in his brown hair shone in the sunlight. As she stared at him, she knew that Philip meant more to her than just an English boy showing her the sights. He had found a permanent place in her heart already, and she couldn't imagine never seeing him again.

"What are you staring at?" he asked self-consciously.

"Oh, nothing. I was thinking. Wishing this afternoon could go on forever . . ."

"What are you doing this evening?"

"We're going to see *Romeo and Juliet* at the Globe." Savannah sat up straighter. "I can't wait."

"I saw it last week—it's terrific. I must have seen that play performed a hundred times, but I never get sick of it."

"Me neither!" Savannah exclaimed.

"You know what, Savannah? I know some of the actors because they come into the pub. How would you like to meet some of them after the performance?" Philip asked.

"Are you serious?" Savannah leaned forward.

"Of course," Philip answered. "I could meet you at the end of the play, and then we could go backstage."

"Can I bring some of my friends?"

"I don't see why not. Not too many though—like three or four. Okay?"

"Oh, my gosh, Philip. Thank you!"

"No problem," he said, laughing as he took another strong pull of the oars.

Thinking about the play, the impulse to recite overcame Savannah. She carefully stood up in the boat and cried, " 'O wonder! How many goodly creatures are there here! How beauteous mankind is! O brave new world . . . !' " She grinned self-consciously at Philip, and he returned her smile.

"You don't know how happy I am to be here," she told him. Savannah gave a slight skip, then stopped abruptly as her feet became tangled in the rope on the bottom of the boat. Trying to regain her footing, she leaned forward to grab the side of the boat, but she missed it. The wild swing of her arm unbalanced her even more and propelled her out of the boat and headfirst into the cold waters of the Avon.

Chapter Eight

The shock of cold water stunned Savannah momentarily. She could hear Philip yelling her name from somewhere far away. More embarrassed than frightened, she hesitated before she swam to the surface. What would Philip think of her?

Well, here goes nothing, Savannah thought. She resurfaced, her hair streaming down her face, laughing and sputtering as she saw Philip's worried expression.

"Savannah, give me your hand," Philip directed as he half pulled and half dragged her back into the boat. "You're not helping," he complained, taking most of her weight as she convulsed with laughter. After a slight struggle, Savannah was safely back in the boat, soaking wet.

"I-I'm sorry," she managed between laughs. "Some date I make. Very romantic." Suddenly, she began shivering as the cold air hit her wet body and clothes.

"Here, take off your jacket and put mine on," Philip suggested.

"I-I'll g-get it all wet," Savannah said, pushing her dripping hair off her face.

"Don't worry about it. I'll row as fast as possible back to the dock and then drive you back to the hostel."

"Thanks." Savannah put the jacket around her shoulders and began picking leaves and grass out of her hair. Looking down, she realized she was creating a puddle in the boat. "I hope I don't have to start bailing soon."

Philip looked down at her feet and then back at her and burst out laughing. "I'm sorry," he apologized. "I was just remembering the shocked look on your face as you tried to grab something before you fell in."

"Are you laughing at me?" Savannah demanded, trying to look stern.

"Yes, I'm sorry," he repeated, blushing.

"Good." Savannah giggled. "I was afraid you might be very angry with me."

"Angry? Why would I be angry? Just a bit concerned, maybe. Though I don't know many girls who fall into rivers and come up laughing!"

"You probably don't know many girls who fall in rivers. You're not embarrassed to be seen with a nut like me?"

"Of course not. What are you talking about? I'm just sorry it happened. This isn't how I imagined the afternoon going." Philip frowned.

"I didn't think you planned this. *Achoo!*" Savannah sneezed.

80

"Please don't get sick. I'd feel terrible if you caught a cold on your vacation."

Savannah shook her head. "I can't believe the messes I always manage to get myself into." The two of them burst out laughing again.

"Achoo!"

"Do you want my shirt?"

"No, I'm fine. I'm just so disappointed—I never got a chance to row," Savannah said.

"Yes, but at least you can say you've been in the Avon River, which is more than I can!"

"That's true." Savannah grinned at him, and their eyes locked for a moment.

"We're here," Philip said. He jumped out onto the dock and quickly tied up the boat. Savannah hurried to follow him, and she was standing beside him before he could help her out. He put his arm around her shoulder and began rubbing it. "It's the least I can do to help keep you warm," he said. "Let's stop at Mrs. Fillingham's bakery—she can lend us a blanket and her car so we don't have to go all the way back to the pub."

Quickly they walked to the bakery. Mrs. Fillingham clucked over Savannah's mishap and insisted on Savannah borrowing her son's clothing.

Savannah came out from the back wearing a pair of oversize pants and a big flannel shirt. She knew she looked ridiculous, but at least she was warmer. Her hair, which had begun to dry, was all snarled.

"And here's a blanket and some hot cocoa to

drink on your ride back to the hostel," Mrs. Fillingham said, handing a cup to Savannah. "Philip Wescott, I'm disappointed in you, letting a young lady fall into the river."

"Mrs. Fillingham, it wasn't his fault. I stood up and rocked the boat, you might say," Savannah explained, giggling at the memory.

"No matter. Philip, don't waste time talking. Get her back to the hostel," the plump woman insisted, shooing them out of the store. "And mind you get my van back to me in top condition."

"Yes, Mrs. Fillingham," Philip said obediently, smiling as he opened the door.

"Thank you, Mrs. Fillingham, for everything. I'll return the clothes as soon as possible. I'll never forget how nice you were," Savannah bubbled, giving her a quick kiss on her cheek.

"I like this girl, Philip Wescott. And tell your ma to come visit!" Mrs. Fillingham called out to them, standing at the bakery door.

Savannah giggled as she and Philip climbed into the bakery van. "I like her. Is she always so . . ."

"Nosy? Pushy?" Philip laughed. "Yes. But she's very generous."

"I *love* this town, Philip. Everyone's been so wonderful. Thanks for showing me around today," Savannah told him.

"Even though you fell into the river?"

"I can't decide if that's the highlight, or whether it was seeing your home, or meeting Mrs. Fillingham. Or maybe it will be the play tonight or meeting the actors afterward. It's all so grand!" she said, putting on an English accent.

82

Savannah started to sing "Jones's Ale," an old English drinking song her grandfather taught her, in her slightly off-key voice. To her surprise and delight, Philip joined in with his rich baritone.

From that song Philip easily moved to another one that Savannah didn't know. Smiling gently, she listened to his soothing voice as he sang about a midsummer morning.

"That's so beautiful and so sad. Sing another one," Savannah requested.

"I don't think I'll have the time today," Philip said as he swung the van down the driveway toward the hostel.

All of a sudden the day seemed less bright to Savannah. "Oh, please don't let Chiochi be there," she whispered to herself.

Philip pulled the van along the front entrance of the hostel. "Here we are, madam."

"Thanks so much, Philip, for a wonderful day. I'll never forget a moment of it."

"Don't think you're getting away this easily! I'm not letting you go in there without me this time. If that ogre is there, we'll greet him together," Philip promised.

Savannah shook her head. "You don't have to do that. I'll be fine on my own."

"I'm sure you will be, but I'm still going in with you," he insisted.

"Okay. Thanks. If Chiochi is there, and it would be just my luck that he is, I could probably use some support," Savannah admitted.

They got out of the van and walked up the

stairs to the front door. For the first time since she had met Philip that morning, Savannah remembered Greg. With a sinking feeling in her stomach, she could imagine his face and what he would say if he saw her like this. If she was lucky, he wouldn't be around.

"Do I look like a complete mess?" Savannah asked Philip.

"Well . . . the blue shirt really brings out the blue in your eyes," Philip offered, smiling at Savannah. "You look fine to me, but I'm afraid you're in no condition to meet the queen."

"Great," Savannah muttered. "Well, here goes."

Savannah opened the big wooden door, and as her eyes adjusted to the darker room, her worst fears were confirmed. Mr. Chiochi was talking to Greg and a few of the other guys. Greg looked handsome and very together in his blue cashmere sweater, jeans, and brown Loafers. When Mr. Chiochi looked up, his look of puzzlement quickly changed to one of concern, and then anger.

"Ms. Wheeler!" he practically barked.

Giving Philip a bleak look, Savannah slowly walked toward the small group. Greg turned around at the sound of her name, but his warm, welcoming smile turned into a frown when he saw Philip.

"What have you done now?" Mr. Chiochi demanded.

"Oh, hello, Mr. Chiochi," Savannah said, trying to appear nonchalant. "I don't think you had a chance to meet Philip Wescott when he dropped me off the other day. Philip, this is Mr. Chiochi, our vice principal. This is Greg Edwards, Howard Holzman, and Tim Norris."

"How do you do, sir," Philip said, coming forward to shake Mr. Chiochi's hand.

Mr. Chiochi couldn't help but take Philip's offered hand. Out of the corner of her eye, Savannah saw Howard and Tim smile.

"Ms. Wheeler, I would *like* an explanation."

Knowing she couldn't avoid him any longer, Savannah took a deep breath and said, "Well, as you know, Mr. Chiochi, today was our free day, where we could explore on our own."

"Did your exploring include a swamp and a used clothing shop, Savannah?" Tim asked, laughing.

"That's enough, Mr. Norris. I am asking the questions. Well, Ms. Wheeler?"

"Philip was kind enough to show me around Stratford," Savannah continued, "which was very educational. This afternoon we were rowing on the Avon. Unfortunately, while rowing—"

"While rowing," Philip quickly interrupted, "I sort of lost control of the oars, sir. To avoid getting hit in the head, Savannah moved forward too quickly and fell into the water. It was all my fault."

Savannah stared at him in mute admiration.

Mr. Chiochi cleared his throat and glanced at Philip, then at Savannah as if questioning the validity of their story. "Well, I suppose I see," he mumbled.

"We docked the boat and went right to Mrs.

Fillingham's bakery. She gave Savannah some of her son's clothing and hot chocolate, and lent us her van so that I could drive Savannah back here before she caught a cold. Savannah was a real trooper about the whole thing. She never once blamed me, sir," Philip said, smiling slightly.

Mr. Chiochi looked doubtful. "Mm-hm. I'm sure she was."

"If you don't mind, Mr. Chiochi, I'd like to change out of these clothes and wash my hair before tonight's play," Savannah said demurely, tucking her hair behind her ears.

"Well, I hope this will be a lesson to both of you. Boat safety is extremely important," Mr. Chiochi warned.

"Oh yes, sir, I know," Savannah said seriously. Tim and Howard laughed loudly.

"This is no laughing matter, gentlemen. These two might have been seriously hurt or worse."

"And," he went on, turning to Savannah, "although today's accident wasn't your fault, I doubt anyone else could land in the Avon. It *would* happen to you." Shaking his head, Mr. Chiochi left the room.

Savannah breathed a sigh of relief and fell back into a chair.

"So, Savannah, what really happened?" Howard asked once Chiochi was out of hearing distance.

Savannah looked up at Howard and noticed that Greg was still standing off to the side, a disapproving look on his face. Sitting up straight in the chair, she realized she must look awful.

Looking first at Savannah, then Greg, and then Savannah again, Philip said, "That's the way it happened, mate. Savannah, I'm going to return Mrs. Fillingham's van now. If you like, you can return the clothes to me tonight at the theater after the play. I'll be there in time to introduce you and your friends to some of the cast."

Savannah jumped out of the chair. "Thanks, Philip, for a great day. It was lots of fun. See you later."

Philip smiled briefly at her, glanced at Greg, and left.

Slowly, Savannah turned around to face the three boys.

"Well, time to change," she said brightly, hoping that Greg would at least say something to her. She touched her hair uncertainly, waiting.

"See you at dinner, Savannah. I'll meet you outside, Tim, Howard," Greg said, brushing by Savannah and walking out the front door.

Looking first at Savannah, then Greg, and
then Savannah again, Billy said. "That's the
way it happened," said Savannah. "I'm going to
follow Mrs. Fillington's plan now. If you like,
you can escort the ladies to the temple at the
theater after the play. I'll be there in time to
surprise you and your friends in some of our
cast."

Savannah jumped out of his chair. "Thanks,
Billy. I'm a great guy. It was jolly of him. See
you later...

Billy smiled sickly, rather, glanced at Greg,
and smiled slowly.

Savannah turned around to face the
three boys.

"Well, time to change," she said firmly, hoping that Greg would understand everything, she
said. She touched her hair once really warmly.
"See you at dinner, Savannah. I'll meet you
outside, Tim. How are," Greg said, brushing by
Savannah and we're in past the downstairs.

Chapter Nine

Practically bouncing in her seat at the Globe Theater, Savannah stared wide-eyed at everything going on around her, from the ushers seating people, to the closed curtains on the stage, to the chandeliers hanging above their heads.

"Stay still, Savannah!" Thea ordered. "You're acting like an overeager puppy."

"Sorry, Thea. But we're here! Finally. And it's so much more beautiful than I imagined."

Thea looked at her carefully. "You're really not upset about Greg, are you?"

"I am, but I decided not to think about it right now. I want to enjoy *Romeo and Juliet*. He and I will talk later. I can't do anything if he's avoiding me, and I'm not going to let it ruin my day or my evening," Savannah stated firmly.

"I wish I could have seen you when you came in this afternoon. According to Howard, it's the first time he ever saw Chiochi speechless in front of you."

Savannah chuckled. "Philip was wonderful, making up that story on the spot. It made me look like the helpless female instead of the cause of the whole mess."

"I'm surprised Greg didn't like that," Thea muttered.

"What?" Savannah asked sharply.

"Oh, nothing. Philip sounds like a great guy."

"He is, Thea. I had the best time with him today. I just wish . . ."

"What?"

"Well, why does he have to live here? He seems like he would be a great friend. After a few days I'll never see him again," Savannah complained.

"You might," Thea said.

"No." Savannah sighed dramatically. "We'll send each other a letter every so often, then only Christmas cards, then nothing. What could have been a great friendship is destined to fade into oblivion."

"Uh-oh, Savannah. Look who's coming this way," Thea whispered, elbowing her.

Savannah looked to her left and noticed Greg scooting over to get to his seat—right next to Savannah.

"I guess it's too late to hide," Savannah whispered. She looked up as Greg reached his seat and smiled brightly at him. Seeing her as though for the first time, he grinned and then busied himself taking off his jacket.

"Hi, Savannah, Thea. Didn't know we'd be sitting next to each other. You both look great," Greg said, although his eyes were only on Savannah, who was wearing an elegant emerald green silk sarong skirt.

"Hi, Greg," Thea said dryly. "Incredible coincidence that we're seated next to you, isn't it?"

Savannah poked Thea and smiled sweetly at Greg. "It's a beautiful theater, don't you think?"

"Yes." Turning his head so his lips were practically at her ear, he whispered, "Savannah, can we talk after the play?"

Savannah moved her head away and looked at him. "Sure. But I'm meeting Philip afterward because he promised to introduce me to some of the actors. Why don't you come along, and then we can talk later?"

Greg hesitated, then nodded. "Thanks, I would like to."

Savannah smiled at him, then turned so that only Thea could see her and stuck her tongue out. Turning back to Greg, she said, "Great. That will be you, Thea, Harry, Emma, and me. Unless Philip says more people can come. . . ."

"Shhh," Thea whispered, hitting Savannah with her program, as the lights dimmed.

When the curtains closed and the lights came up for intermission after the third act, Savannah was still crying.

"Savannah, what is it?" Greg asked.

"It's all so beautiful and tragic."

"It's only a play," Greg stated practically.

"I know it's only a play. I'm not stupid." The words flew out of Savannah's mouth before she could stop them. She and Greg just stared at each other for a moment.

"I'm sorry, Savannah. I guess it just doesn't get to me as much as it does to you," Greg admitted.

"Well I can't help it. Movies, books, and plays can really affect me."

"Hey, guys, you want to walk around a bit?" Madeleine asked. She was sitting on the other side of Thea.

"Sure. Besides, I have to ask Ms. Martin about taking some time after the show to meet the actors," Savannah said, standing. "Do you want to come, Greg?"

"Sure."

"Thea, you coming?"

"No. I'm going to see what's happening with Harry." She grinned.

Greg and Savannah followed Madeleine and found Ms. Martin in the upstairs lobby, talking with Elaine and Howard.

"Ms. Martin, isn't it *wonderful*?" Savannah asked.

"I thought you'd be enjoying this." Ms. Martin smiled at Savannah's shining eyes. "Not quite the same as doing it in class, is it?"

Madeleine laughed. "That's for sure. Shakespeare sounds a lot better with an English accent than a Boston accent!"

"Ms. Martin, my friend Philip has offered to introduce some of us to the actors after the performance. Would that be okay with you?" Savannah asked.

"It does sound like a great opportunity, but it seems unfair to me that only some people will get to enjoy it," Ms. Martin replied.

"I agree, but I couldn't ask him to take all eighteen of us when he offered. He said only a few people, but when I meet him after the play, I'll ask if more can come along."

"How did you decide who was going to join you in this treat?" Ms. Martin inquired.

"I already asked Thea, Harry, Greg, and Emma, mostly because they were around. I didn't know how else to do it. I'm sorry, Madeleine and Howard," Savannah explained.

"Well, I don't see any problem if you promise to stay only an extra fifteen minutes and then go straight to the hostel. I do wish the whole class could be there, though."

"I'll ask Philip, but I'm sure he'll have to okay it with the actors. I just can't imagine that after a night's performance, they'll want so many people descending on them."

"Did I hear you say you can't imagine something, Ms. Wheeler?" Mr. Chiochi asked, coming up behind the group. "That's surely a first."

Savannah shot Ms. Martin a worried look.

"Savannah has been fortunate enough to be invited with a few others to meet some of the actors backstage. I've already given her permission," Ms. Martin explained, not giving the vice principal a chance to object. "I'll wait up for them."

"I'll see if we can get the whole class to come," Savannah promised. "I'm meeting him in the lobby right after the play."

"We're all meeting there, so we'll find out what's going on then. I hear the warning bells—

we'd best get back to our seats," Ms. Martin instructed.

"You handled that very smoothly," Greg commented softly as he and Savannah went back to their seats. She just smiled at him.

After the play the class met in the front lobby. Philip was waiting there already, talking with one of the ushers. When he saw Savannah, he quickly finished talking with his friend and went right over to her. "Hi, enjoy the play?"

Still overcome with the quality of the production, Savannah just smiled and nodded.

"Look, I realized after I saw you that it wouldn't really be fair to select only a few people, so I called up Jeff—he played Mercutio—and he said they'd be willing to talk to the whole class."

Savannah gasped with delight. "Oh, thank you, Philip! Ms. Martin said it was fine, but she wasn't pleased only a few of us would get to do this. Come with me and tell her." She grabbed his hand and pulled him over to Ms. Martin, who was standing with Mr. Chiochi. "Ms. Martin, Philip's arranged it so we can *all* talk to the actors! Isn't that great?"

"That's wonderful. Thank you, Philip. I appreciate your going to all this trouble," Ms. Martin told him.

"No trouble for me at all. It's the people in the play who are being so generous," Philip explained. "They told me they would come and get us, and then we can go back into the theater and talk with them for a short while."

"Mr. Chiochi, don't you think it's lovely that Philip and Savannah have arranged this extra treat?" Ms. Martin asked pointedly.

"Yes. Thank you," Mr. Chiochi said with a small nod.

"Philip, they're ready for you now," an usher said, coming up to the small group.

"Class, we're going back into the theater to talk with some of the actors," Ms. Martin announced.

Quickly, the class entered the theater. Sitting at the foot of the stage in their costumes and makeup were the actors who had played Mercutio, Juliet, the nurse, and the friar.

Madeleine groaned. "Why couldn't Romeo be here? He was just too hot."

"I'm surprised at you, Ms. Sheldon. We are here for an educational experience," Savannah teased.

"You might be, but I'm here on a purely amateur level," Madeleine retorted. "On the other hand, Mercutio is sort of cute. . . ."

"You're hopeless." Thea shook her head, grinning.

The class sat in the first two rows and started asking questions about the play and life in the theater in general. Although Greg and Savannah ended up sitting in different rows, she could feel him looking at her.

After twenty minutes Jeff, the actor who played Mercutio, stood up. "I'm afraid we're exhausted, so we're going to call it a night," he announced. "Thanks for coming to the play and for paying so much attention. We only wish all our audiences were so enthusiastic!"

"Thank you very much for giving us more of your time," Ms. Martin said, after the class stood and applauded the actors.

"Philip, do you need a ride home?" Ms. Martin offered as they headed to the bus.

"Sure, thanks. If it's on your way."

Greg, Savannah, Elaine, Harry, Philip, and Thea boarded the bus, rushing toward the back so they could sit far away from Mr. Chiochi. Savannah found herself sitting between Greg and Philip, without planning it at all.

"Philip, that was so interesting. Thanks so much," Elaine said.

"It was the neatest," Thea said.

"It was fun for me too. And great to get away from the pub for a while. Hey, do you guys know about the legend of Shakespeare's ghost?"

"No," Savannah said, leaning forward. "Tell us."

"When the moon is full, around midnight, his ghost is supposed to appear in town," Philip explained.

"I've never heard that before." Greg looked skeptical.

"It's true. A friend of my father's saw him in the garden of Ann Hathaway's house. Do you want to go?" Philip asked. "There'll be a full moon in two nights."

"Oh, let's," Savannah urged the others.

"The hostel is closed at eleven, Savannah. We wouldn't be allowed," Elaine pointed out.

"Details, details. You've got to live a little, Elaine. Take risks," Savannah encouraged her. "We can sneak out. I say we go for it."

"I don't know, Philip. This sounds like a dumb story that you tell to naive tourists," Greg argued.

"Would I kid you guys?" Philip asked. "Actually, it's something we hardly tell *anyone*. The locals don't want the town filled with more reporters and tourists than it already is."

"Well, count me out," Elaine said flatly. "I don't want to get in trouble because of some silly stunt." The others didn't reply.

"Well, if anyone's interested, I'm game. Ms. Martin, this is my stop!" Philip called out, standing. He looked down at Savannah briefly, but said to everyone, "This was fun. It was nice to meet you all." Savannah watched as he walked down the aisle of the bus, said good night to the two teachers, and got off the bus.

Fifteen minutes later they pulled up to the hostel.

"Tomorrow we'll be sightseeing again as a group, so I expect to see everyone at breakfast bright and early," Mr. Chiochi said as they filed off the bus. They all nodded sleepily and headed for their rooms.

"Savannah, wait," Greg whispered, holding on to her sleeve. "There are no rules that say we have to go to bed when everyone else does. I'd like to talk with you."

"That sounds good," she agreed shyly. Savannah looked at him questioningly as they both sat down on the couch.

"Savannah, almost since this trip first started, we've had nothing but misunderstandings. We weren't like this in Boston," Greg began.

Savannah nodded. "I know."

"You seem so different here. You and Chiochi have run-ins every day. And then this afternoon you come in with someone else's clothes on, dripping wet. I mean, who ever heard of someone falling into the Avon?"

"Don't you believe me?" Savannah asked, her voice rising.

"Shhh—do you want them to come out here? Of course I believe you, but face it, it didn't happen to anyone but you."

"What are you trying to say, Greg?"

"I'm saying it all wrong. When I saw you come in with that guy—"

"Philip?" Savannah asked cooly.

"Yeah, Philip. It's just that when you two came in together, I got so jealous. I don't want you going out with him. He looks at you in a way that just makes me furious."

"You mean, you weren't angry with me?" Savannah asked.

"No, not really. I was just worried when I saw you getting into another argument with Chiochi."

"Then why didn't you look at me? You acted as if I had done something wrong," Savannah said, surprised that Greg was jealous of Philip. She never thought of herself as the type of girl someone would be jealous over. She felt a momentary thrill. And yet, she also couldn't ignore the fact that Greg often disapproved of her be-

98

havior because it made him look bad, or that he sometimes seemed to think she was there merely to reflect well on him because they were a couple. She didn't know what feeling inside her was the strongest: happiness because he was jealous or anger because he thought he could tell her what she should or shouldn't do. *I don't even know if I like him anymore,* Savannah realized to herself.

"I just hate it when the girl I'm going out with gets involved in crazy escapades," Greg continued. "It's so embarrassing. Like this thing with Shakespeare's ghost—come on, Savannah! Anyone can see that he was joking. And you were acting as if you would really do it!"

"I was just joking too," she lied. "I knew it couldn't be true."

"Savannah," Greg said, taking her hands in his, "I really like being with you. Don't let Philip or anything else get between us, okay?" Slowly, he pulled her toward him and kissed her softly on the lips. "Please don't get involved with him in any more crazy schemes."

"I won't," Savannah promised, crossing her fingers behind her back.

"That's my girl," he said, kissing her again.

Chapter Ten

" 'That's my girl!' That's what he said? And you fell for it?" Thea exclaimed the next morning when the two friends were alone in the girls' bathroom.

"I knew you would react this way," Savannah mumbled, around her toothbrush.

"Well, what do you expect? He talks to you like you're seven years old. How would you like it if Chiochi said that to you?"

Savannah quickly rinsed out her mouth. "I agree with you, Thea. I listen to more nonsense from Greg than I do from anyone else. But I vowed that I would behave in front of him, and that includes not letting him see my weird side."

"But why?" Thea demanded. "That's you!"

Savannah made a wry face. "Thanks a lot." She was silent as she brushed her hair. "I like him. He's incredibly good-looking, he's the most popular boy in our school, and he likes me too."

"So? Lots of people like you," Thea said as

she put mascara on her blond lashes. "What about Philip?"

Savannah shrugged. "He's great. We had a lot of fun yesterday. I felt so comfortable with him, I even told him about my grandfather," she admitted, laughing at Thea's surprised face. "We sang in the van on the way back to the hostel. And you guys were right—he is really cute. Not handsome like Greg, but adorable cute. But he lives here, so it just doesn't make sense to think about him as a boyfriend. And out of everyone I know in Boston, Greg's the best guy for me."

"For a romantic, you have a real practical streak in you," Thea observed wryly.

"I have to be somewhat realistic. And if I have to be a certain way to keep Greg interested in me, I will. I'm certainly learning to control myself around him and not always rushing off to do the first thing that comes into my head. I think that's important."

"I hope you know what you're doing, Savannah. All I hear are the incredibly stupid things Greg says, and then you defend him and get annoyed with me for thinking he's an idiot," Thea commented.

"I know. I'm sorry, Thea. You've been a real pal putting up with it. Let's not talk about Greg for at least ten minutes, okay? How's life with Harry?"

Thea smiled broadly and put down her brush. "He's a riot. He's so shy that most people don't know he's funny, but he is. And sweet. He also thinks Greg is a jerk."

Savannah twirled around and faced Thea. "What have you been telling him?"

"Nothing. But he has eyes and ears. Everyone knows you two are a couple. He doesn't think Greg treats you right. You're so smart and independent, and he treats you like you don't have a mind of your own. Harry also thinks it's strange that you don't spend more time together. You spent your free day with Philip, and Greg spent his with Elaine."

"That's fine with me," Savannah said defiantly. "We're allowed to have our friends."

Although she defended Greg to Thea, Savannah was angry and hurt inside. Greg had made her feel incredibly guilty about going out with Philip, but he had gone out with Elaine all day and hadn't even mentioned it! *Why did he act as if I was the only one who spent the day with someone of the opposite sex?* Savannah thought to herself. *And why do I always feel like I've done something wrong when I'm around Greg?*

Suddenly Savannah noticed that Thea was watching her. She laughed lightly and asked, "Are you finished putting your goop on yet?"

"Savannah, you must be patient," Thea explained. "Not everyone has naturally long curled lashes and rosy cheeks."

"Yes, I'm such a natural beauty," Savannah joked, flipping her hair back over her shoulder. She stared at herself in the mirror. "Thea, do you really think I'm okay? You and Elaine are so pretty."

"Don't you dare compare me to her," Thea threatened holding her hairbrush menacingly above Savannah's head.

"I didn't mean you look alike. But both of you have such classic good looks, I look like—"

"Absolutely adorable. I will be a faded beauty by the time I'm thirty, but you, Savannah, will still be the belle of the ball," Thea said dramatically.

"Let's go eat, you dope." Savannah laughed. "You'll never fade—your mouth is too big!"

Thea hit her with a towel, and the two girls laughed as they headed down the hallway to breakfast. When they entered the dining room, they saw that Harry and Greg were sitting together and had saved them seats.

"You know, if nothing else, we've been instrumental in getting those two to know each other," Savannah commented as they waved at the boys.

The two girls got their food and sat down next to the boys. Savannah thought Greg looked even more handsome than usual in a crisp white button-down shirt and chinos.

"Did you know that you two are always the last ones to come to breakfast? What do you do back there?" Harry asked.

"It's Thea's fault. She has to try on five different outfits before she's ready," Savannah teased.

"I might change my clothes a lot, but it's Savannah's false teeth that take so much time," Thea countered, sticking her tongue out at her friend.

"Yeah? Well—"

Mr. Chiochi stood up and blew his whistle,

interrupting Savannah's retort. "Ms. Martin has an announcement," he stated, sitting back down.

"Thank you, Mr. Chiochi," Ms. Martin said, trying not to smile. "Tomorrow is May first, which is May Day. That's a special day here, and in Stratford they are celebrating by having a dawn dance with a maypole and morris dancers. Who here would like to go and watch it? It means getting up very, very early."

Immediately Savannah's hand shot up. Thea's, Harry's, Howard's, and a few others were next. Eventually Greg also raised his hand.

"Great. What about the rest of you sleepyheads?" Ms. Martin asked. "How can you come all the way to England and not take advantage of everything that is here?" The class groaned in response. "The rest of you can tell me tonight. I just need to let the bus driver know to be here early tomorrow since a number of you definitely want to go." She counted hands again and sat back down.

"Isn't this wild?" Savannah exclaimed, turning to her friends. "I've always wanted to dance around a maypole. And to do it here in England —what could be better?"

"How early does this mean we have to get up?" Greg groaned.

"Greg, get into it!" Thea laughed. "Probably around four A.M. No big thing—we're on vacation."

"What *is* morris dancing, anyway?" Savannah asked, embarrassed that there were some things about England she still didn't know.

105

"Traditional English ritual dancing. It's cool," Harry informed them.

"How do you know?" Thea asked, turning to him.

"My cousin does it back home. They wear white and have bells strapped to their shins. They dance with hankies or sticks, depending on which tradition they're following. It's probably more fun to do than to watch, but it will be neat to see real Englishmen do it."

"What about the women?" Savannah asked.

"I knew that would upset Savannah!" Greg laughed. The other three ignored his comment. Savannah and Thea looked at Harry for an answer.

"It's traditionally a man's dance. I don't know what they do here, but I know there are women's groups in the States," Harry said. "I've never seen a maypole dance."

"I hope we can join in," Savannah said fervently.

"I doubt anyone could stop you," Thea teased.

Greg was about to say something when Mr. Chiochi blew his whistle, signaling the clean-up crew to get started, while the others got ready to leave for their day in Oxford.

The class arrived in Oxford late in the morning, and for the first few hours they followed a local tour guide, seeing the different colleges. After a late lunch Ms. Martin told everyone that they could spend the next four hours however they wished and that they were to meet back at the bus at six-thirty.

Savannah, Greg, Harry, Thea, Elaine, and Howard quickly formed a group to decide what to do.

"There were some beautiful gardens I would love to go back to," Savannah suggested.

"No," Howard objected. "Let's check out the pubs."

"No, we can't," Elaine argued. "I like the garden idea."

"What about renting some boats? That way we can pass by the gardens and see more of Oxford," Harry suggested.

"That's a great idea," Thea said instantly.

"Sounds good to me," Savannah agreed, looking at Harry with respect.

"Only this time you won't have a problem staying in the boat with me rowing, Savannah," Greg teased.

The others laughed, but Savannah remained quiet, upset that Greg would make fun of her that way. She didn't appreciate the way he had insulted Philip, either, after everything he had done for her.

"Don't listen to him, Savannah," Harry said to her privately as the group walked toward the river.

"Thanks, Harry. I don't really mind being teased, but it wasn't Philip's fault that I landed in the river. It was mine, and he took the blame to keep me out of trouble. I feel bad not coming to his defense," she explained.

"I'm sure he wouldn't mind. After all, he made up the story because he wanted to cover for

107

you. And I doubt he would be bothered by some joking," Harry assured her.

Savannah gave him a steady look. "You know, Harry, it's nice to finally get to know you. Of course, if you mistreat Thea, I'll have to beat you up, but I doubt you will."

"Hey, what are you two talking about?" Thea asked, waiting for them to catch up to the group. "Don't believe a word she says, Harry."

"I was just telling him about the time in sleep-away camp when you had that crush on Rick."

"Savannah! You didn't! I'll never speak to you again!" Thea shrieked.

"See you later!" Savannah laughed, running up to Greg.

"What was that all about?" Greg asked as she joined him.

"Nothing really. I just mentioned a certain camp counselor," Savannah answered, looking back and watching Thea shake her head violently and laugh. "Thea had this intense crush on this fifteen-year-old camp counselor when she was eight years old, and she would follow him everywhere. We got into so much trouble because we missed all our activities just to be near Rick. We were kicked out of camp. Our parents were furious."

"I can't believe you would tell Harry about that. Thea never acts silly now," Greg commented.

Savannah looked at Greg. Did he mean that *she* was the only one capable of being silly now? "It was just something funny that happened at camp," she explained again. "I was only teasing her."

Greg shrugged. "Whatever. There's Howard. Looks like he already has the information about the boats."

Howard waited until everyone joined him before saying, "We can rent boats, but only the ones for two people. They don't have any more of the larger ones. So we have to split up."

Savannah saw Thea and Harry smile at each other when they thought no one was looking, and she was surprised at the jealousy she felt. Suddenly, being alone in a boat with Greg didn't seem as much fun as it might have a week ago.

The group split up, agreeing to stay within shouting distance of one another.

"I'm glad there's only room for two in a boat, aren't you?" Greg asked as he took the oars and rowed the boat out to the center of the river.

Savannah quickly smiled and nodded. "Oxford is beautiful. All the steeples and old, old buildings. And I just love English gardens, don't you?"

"Hmmm. Why are you so taken with England?" Greg asked.

She looked at him and then down at the water. "It's because of my grandfather, I guess. He used to tell me stories about growing up here, and I just—"

"Savannah, look!" Greg interrupted, pointing. "Isn't that Chiochi standing up there?"

"Greg, I was just—"

"Look, quickly. Before he goes inside!" Greg

insisted. "Hey, Howard, Harry, isn't that Chiochi?"

Everyone turned, following Greg's finger. Atop one of the spired buildings stood their vice principal, his whistle gleaming in the sunlight.

"He looks so small and alone," Savannah mused quietly, standing to get a better view.

"Savannah, sit down or you'll tip the boat," Greg commanded. "Don't be so stupid."

Stung, she sat down quickly with her hands folded. *Be calm*, she told herself. *Things will just get worse if you tell him off.* Looking around, she saw Thea and Harry laughing as they tried to row at the same time with separate oars. They kept going around in circles, but they didn't care. She envied their easygoing happiness. "Sorry," she murmured. "I didn't mean to cause trouble."

"It's okay," Greg replied. "Chiochi looked so funny up there, don't you think?"

Savannah shrugged. "I guess."

They rowed in silence for a few minutes. Watching Elaine, Savannah saw her sitting perfectly still, allowing Howard to row, making comments about the scenery they passed. Savannah knew that if she acted properly like Elaine, Greg wouldn't constantly tell her what *not* to do. *But you'd suffocate*, she realized quietly.

"Your hair looks beautiful in the sunlight," Greg observed. "All golden red."

Savannah looked at him. His arm muscles were taut as they pulled the oars, his hair fell casually over his forehead, and there was a fine

110

sheen of sweat on his face. When he grinned at her, her stomach dropped. He looked so good!

"Why don't we row together?" she said, moving carefully to his seat so she wouldn't rock the boat. They squeezed closer together, and she took one of the oars. Following his rhythm, she began pulling the oar. A gentle breeze lifted her hair off her neck, and she gave a contented sigh. "This is nice."

"Savannah, don't pull so hard. You'll make the boat go around in circles," Greg instructed.

"Greg, why don't you—"

"Harry! Stop!" Thea shrieked. Savannah looked over and saw Harry purposely splashing Thea with an oar. Thea reached into the water and splashed him with her hand. The two of them were laughing hysterically.

Savannah took a deep breath. Thea's shriek had stopped her from saying anything nasty to Greg.

"They're so dumb," Greg said, shaking his head.

"Looks like fun to me," Savannah said flatly. "Let's get back to rowing now."

"Don't be silly, Savannah. I should be doing this."

"Greg Edwards, I'm just as capable of rowing as you are," Savannah insisted.

"Come on, you don't see Elaine or even Thea insisting on rowing. Don't be so difficult," Greg said in an irritated voice.

Holding the oar tightly so she wouldn't say anything she'd regret, Savannah looked over at

111

Elaine. She was sitting in the same spot, in the same position, pulling her blond hair back with one hand while holding onto the boat with the other. She looked calm, cool, in control. Not angry irritated, or hot as Savannah felt.

"Why don't you sit back where you were and let me be the captain of this vessel?" Greg suggested with a wink.

Savanna obeyed his orders and sat in the front of the boat, positioning her body just like Elaine's. "Beautiful weather today," she commented, feeling ridiculous, but knowing anything she *really* wanted to say would start a fight.

Greg smiled at her appreciatively. "You look so pretty sitting there like that."

"Thank you," she said politely. Savannah thought quickly, *What would Elaine say right now?* "Are you having a good time on this trip?" she asked.

"It's great to get out of school. If we were back home, I wouldn't be in a boat with my girlfriend in the middle of the day like this. I love it!" Greg exclaimed.

Savannah glanced over at Thea and Harry. With his pants rolled up, Harry's feet trailed in the water while Thea rowed, splashing him now and then with the oars. Her familiar giggles echoed, and Savannah wished she was with them . . . or with Philip on his boat.

"Greg, Harry, it's time to head back now!" Elaine called, pointing to her watch.

"Not so soon," Harry groaned.

"In order for us to get back to the bus on time, we need to turn around now," Elaine said primly. "That way we don't have to run back to the bus."

"What's wrong with running?" Savannah muttered under her breath.

But everyone headed back to shore and arrived at the bus in plenty of time. Ms. Martin was waiting for them.

"What did you six do?" she asked as they boarded the bus.

"Rowed down the Isis," Harry said, grinning.

"I've always wanted to do that. How was it, Savannah?"

"I think I liked the Avon better," she said quietly.

in order for us to get back to the bus on time," I used to learn around now," Elaine said patiently. "But now when I have to run back to the bus."

"That's wrong with running?" a small muttered under her breath.

But everyone headed back to shore and as two of the boys in ... Jenny of ... Merweather was waiting for them.

"What did you do?" she asked as they boarded the bus.

"Rowed down the lake," Her ... girl, grinning. "I've always wanted to do that. How was it ..."

"I think I liked the ... even better," she said quietly.

Chapter Eleven

Savannah sat near the window on the bus the next morning, peering eagerly through the mist. Beside her Greg groaned in protest against the early hour. She glanced at him briefly and smiled, remembering the kisses they had shared the night before. Her smile changed to a grimace as her thoughts turned to the boat trip in Oxford.

Maybe if we never talk to each other and only kiss, we'll be fine together, Savannah thought to herself.

"Do you have to be so bouncy this early in the morning?" Greg complained.

"Sorry, I guess I'm more of a morning person than you are. I also can't wait to see the maypole."

"I hope this is worth it," Greg grumbled.

Savannah kept her mouth shut, knowing that in his grumpy mood, Greg would disagree with whatever she said. Behind her, Thea and Harry were whispering and giggling together. Savannah sighed, looking at Greg's tired face. He

115

looked great, but he sure wasn't her idea of true love anymore.

The bus wound its way toward town and passed the pasture that she and Philip had crossed.

Philip. She wondered if she would see him again before they left for London and then home. Staring out the window, she saw his grin with his slightly crooked teeth, his light brown straight hair sticking up awkwardly, and his sky blue eyes. Savannah giggled out loud.

"What's so funny?" Greg asked, his eyes barely opening.

"Nothing. Go back to sleep." There was no way Savannah could explain to him that she was thinking of Philip!

The driver turned onto the main street of town and parked the bus. The class groggily left the bus and followed Ms. Martin and Mr. Chiochi to the village green.

"Oh, look!" Savannah exclaimed.

In the center of the green was a tall pole, and hanging from the top were wide, brightly colored ribbons. Some children were already pulling at the ribbons and running around each other in a mock maypole dance, while their parents tried to catch them.

To the right of the pole were men dressed in white, with bells and ribbons sewn on their outfits. Six of them were already dancing with hankies, jumping and turning. Two other men in white were playing instruments, a recorder and a concertina.

116

Savannah clapped her hands together. "I love it! Come on, let's get closer." She took Greg's and Thea's hands and dragged them toward the pole, with Harry following.

"It's Miss Savannah, isn't it?" a familiar voice asked.

She turned and saw George. "George, hi! Why aren't you dancing?"

"My knees can't take it anymore. Who are these folks?" George asked, gesturing with his unlit pipe.

"These are my friends, Thea, Harry, and Greg. Guys, this is George. He's one of the men I met in the pub my first day here. It seems like such a long, long time ago. I'll have to come in for some more of Philip's mom's cider before we leave."

"Speaking of Philip, do you recognize any of those dancers?" George asked, smiling.

Savannah looked back at the dancers and noticed that one of the men seemed to be jumping higher than the rest.

"Thea, it's Philip!" Savannah watched him intently as he did the intricate steps and twirls.

"They're great," Harry said.

"I love the music," Thea commented. "Don't you, Greg?"

Greg shrugged. "It's okay. Give me rock 'n' roll any day, though."

"Oh, Greg, don't be such a party pooper," Thea said as she turned back to the dancers.

When the dance was over, Savannah ran over to Philip. "You didn't tell me you'd be here! You were great!" she said, squeezing his arm.

117

"Savannah! I thought you might be here. It's so good to see you." Philip smiled widely, staring at her.

"I've missed you," she said before she could stop herself. "I mean—"

"I've missed you too," he said quietly.

They stood there for a few moments, just staring into each other's eyes.

"Philip, you're on again!" one of the dancers called.

Philip shifted from foot to foot. He seemed nervous about something. "Savannah, remember what I told you about Shakespeare's ghost?" he asked. "Tonight's the night—do you want to wait with me to see him?"

"I—I . . ." she hesitated, looking back over her shoulder at Greg. "Yes, of course."

"Great! Meet me down at the end of the drive of the hostel at eleven-thirty tonight. I'll bring whatever we need," Philip promised. Walking backward, still looking at her, he joined the other dancers, only turning away from her when the dance started. Savannah went back to her friends.

"You two seem to be very friendly," Greg observed.

"That's because we're friends, Greg," Savannah replied sharply. She didn't like his possessive tone. "There's nothing wrong with being friendly, is there?"

"No, I didn't say there was. I'm just tired."

"I'm sorry I snapped at you," Savannah answered. She was beginning to realize that lately anything Greg said rubbed her the wrong way.

118

"Savannah, the maypole dance is starting," Thea said excitedly as she and Harry headed over to join the other dancers.

"Greg, do you want to dance? It might wake you up," Savannah said as nicely as she could.

"No, you go ahead. I'll just watch."

"Okay." Savannah ran to catch up with Thea and Harry. They each took a ribbon and followed the caller's instructions, creating an elaborate spider web. Then they danced again to undo it.

"I'm hot," Savannah told Thea as they went back to join Greg.

"Look, another dance is starting," Thea said. The two girls turned around and noticed that more people were grabbing hold of ribbons to dance again.

Impulsively, Savannah pulled off her shoes. "I have to dance again. Do you want to?"

"Of course," Thea said, grinning. "This is so much fun!"

"Greg, come join us!" Savannah called. He shook his head and stayed where he was. "Well, watch my shoes then."

"Savannah, you want to share a ribbon?" Philip asked, coming up to them. "We're on a break."

"You don't need to ask twice."

They shared a ribbon, and the new dance created a basketlike pattern out of the ribbons.

"Isn't that your vice principal?" Philip asked as they began to do the dance to untangle the ribbons.

Savannah looked over and saw Mr. Chiochi watching the dancing. To her surprise he actually looked as if he were enjoying himself. His feet were tapping to the rhythm of the music.

Savannah had a sudden inspiration. "Philip, would you mind if I asked him to dance with me? Despite the fact that he's a stick-in-the-mud, there's something kind of sweet about him. And he looks like he really wants to join in."

He looked down at her thoughtfully. "It would be a shame if you didn't ask him, then."

"Save this ribbon," Savannah said, running over to Mr. Chiochi. "Mr. Chiochi, would you like to dance? We'll have to share a ribbon because there aren't enough. A friend of mine is saving one for us."

"Ms. Wheeler," he began sternly. "I . . . I would love to."

Without thinking, Savannah grabbed the vice principal's arm. His clipboard flew out of his hand.

"I'm s-so sorry, Mr. Chiochi," Savannah stuttered. "I didn't mean to do that."

"It's quite all right, Ms. Wheeler. It's only a clipboard. Now, where is that ribbon?"

Grinning, Savannah pointed, and together they walked over to Philip, who had continued dancing.

"My replacement, I see," Philip teased, letting go of the ribbon. Savannah and Mr. Chiochi took his place and began to weave in and out, passing by the other dancers.

Thrilled that she and Mr. Chiochi were finally involved in something other than a fight, Savannah glanced at her vice principal, and they both shared a smile, then danced right into the couple ahead of them. Moving out of their way, Mr. Chiochi and Savannah went under the next ribbon instead of over, changing the whole pattern. Instead of untangling the basket, the ribbons became more snarled.

"Way to go, Savannah!" she heard Danny Cassorla call out.

"I guess I did it again, huh, Mr. Chiochi?" Savannah said as everyone started dancing in different directions, laughing and singing as they did.

"I guess you did," Mr. Chiochi agreed. "But you know what, Savannah? It's a lot more fun this way!"

Chapter Twelve

"Savannah, you shouldn't do this," Thea whispered as Savannah put her clothes on in the girls' bathroom that night.

"I know I shouldn't, but I want to," she whispered back, pulling a heavy sweater over her head. "Besides, what could possibly happen? The pillows look like a body under the covers. When I come back, I'll knock softly on the window, and you'll let me in."

"These things have a way of backfiring, Savannah."

"Don't worry. Chiochi can't do anything to me. I'll blackmail him—he did dance without his shoes on, you know." Savannah giggled. "Come on, you've got to lock the front door after me."

The two girls crept down the hallway to the main room. Everyone else was asleep, tired from having woken up so early. Savannah was too excited to feel exhausted. Carefully, she unlocked the front door, gave Thea a quick hug, and went outside to meet Philip.

Alone under the full moon, the driveway suddenly didn't seem familiar to Savannah. She thought she saw strange shapes behind the trees that lined the drive. The night noises were louder than she remembered.

Regretting she had ever agreed to meet Philip, Savannah felt a cold hand grab her shoulder and another cold hand cover her mouth.

"It's me, Philip," he whispered behind her, letting her go.

"You sc-scared me to death!" Savannah gasped.

"Sorry, but I thought you'd scream if I jumped out in front of you," Philip explained. "I couldn't come up with any other method. Next time I'll know, okay?"

She shook her head, grinning slightly. "Okay."

"I brought Godiva and the wagon. I figured that would be the quietest way to travel. And you missed most of your first ride by sleeping!" Philip reminded her as they reached the wagon.

"Very thoughtful of you," Savannah said, climbing up on the wagon.

They reached Ann Hathaway's house about ten minutes later. Philip parked the wagon behind a shed, took a bundle out of the wagon, and led Savannah into the garden. Then he stopped and spread out a blanket he had brought, and motioned for Savannah to sit down. From his knapsack he produced a thermos and two mugs. He poured them each a steaming cup of hot chocolate.

Savannah sipped it and smiled at him. "It's delicious."

"A secret family recipe. I'll save some for later. Here, I brought more blankets if we need them."

"You've thought of everything," Savannah said, holding the mug close to her face. "Morris dancing looks so neat. I'll have to look for it when I get back to Boston. Harry says there are teams of people who do it at home."

Philip grinned. "Your calling a maypole dance was one of the funniest things I've ever seen."

"It didn't embarrass you?"

"Are you kidding? You would have had it perfectly if you had said 'over' instead of 'under' that one time. I've never seen someone catch on to creating patterns as quickly."

"Thanks."

They were quiet for a few moments, drinking their hot chocolate. Savannah sighed happily.

"Missing your grandfather?"

"No." Savannah sat up straighter, startled.

"What is it?"

"How can you tell that there's anything bothering me?" she asked.

"You get very still and quiet when there's something you want to say or ask and you don't know how," Philip answered. She looked at him. "I've watched you," he explained, shrugging his shoulders.

"Did you think I was silly when I told you that stuff about my grandfather?" Savannah asked.

"Savannah, you may be funny sometimes, but you're never silly, or at least not foolish. My grandmother means a lot to me—we're very close," Philip told her. "Why would it be silly for you to love your grandfather so much?"

"I don't know," she answered quietly. "I started to mention it to someone else, and I just felt dumb."

"Then it was that person's problem, not yours."

"You are the neatest person I ever met, Philip Wescott. I wish I didn't have to go home," Savannah said truthfully.

"You really have to go back, don't you?" His voice sounded sad.

"I don't want to," Savannah said urgently. "I feel like I belong here. Everyone is just so wonderful. I just mentioned to George this morning that I wanted to taste your mum's cider again, and then there he was, with enough for everyone."

"It doesn't surprise me that he did that," Philip said, taking her hand. "I mean, you just enjoy everything so much, I want to keep showing you things just to make you happy."

"Philip, I—"

He leaned closer to her and kissed her gently on the lips. Gasping slightly, she kissed him back.

"Savannah, I wish you didn't have to leave." he murmured, kissing her again.

Savannah opened her eyes to make sure she wasn't imagining the whole scene. Looking beyond Philip's head, she saw a big dark shape moving closer to them.

"It's him, Philip!" she screamed. "It's Shakespeare!"

Philip jumped up, knocking over the mugs of chocolate. "Where, Savannah, where?"

She pointed with a shaky hand.

"Stay here," he whispered.

"No way are you leaving me alone," she hissed back, standing up and grabbing hold of his jacket.

Together they crept closer to the black shadow. It didn't seem to be moving. Suddenly Philip burst out laughing.

"What is it? What's so funny?"

"Savannah, it's the fountain, not a ghost." He shone his flashlight on the stone fountain in the center of the garden.

"But it looked like it was moving," Savannah insisted.

"Maybe the shadows from the trees made it look that way," Philip suggested.

"Well, it certainly scared me. You know, maybe we shouldn't stick around to see this ghost after all."

"Uh, Savannah . . ." Philip said as they sat back down on a dry section of the chocolate-soaked blanket, "I have a confession to make. But first you have to promise me you won't be angry."

"I can't really promise until I know what it is," Savannah argued.

"Well, okay. Look. There is no ghost of Shakespeare. I made up the whole legend."

"Oh. I see," she said stiffly.

"I just wanted to spend some time with you, and you're leaving soon," Philip explained, sounding more unsure of himself than she had ever heard him before.

"So the famous Stratford ghost is a figment

of your imagination," Savannah said, not looking at him.

"You *are* angry."

Savannah turned toward him, her face stern. Suddenly she broke into peals of laughter. "Philip, if you could see your face! I knew the ghost wasn't real. I'm not *that* silly." She rolled over on the blanket, laughing.

"Savannah!" Philip shook her, starting to laugh himself.

She rolled over so she was facing him. "Well, actually, I was pretty naive. I believed you until today, when I told George that I was going to see the ghost. He had no idea what I was talking about, so I knew you had made it up."

"Then why did you agree to come out here?" he asked.

"You're not the only one who wanted us to spend more time together," she answered, looking up into his eyes.

He leaned down and kissed her.

"You know, you could have just asked me," Savannah said softly.

"I didn't know what your friend Greg would have said."

Savannah sat up and hugged her knees to her chest. "He wouldn't have liked it very much. He would hate it if he knew I was here."

They were silent for a moment. "You two are going with each other, aren't you?" Philip finally asked.

"Yes, I guess so, but . . . it's so complicated. I thought he was the one I wanted, but it just

128

isn't working out. I thought it would be okay to be the way he wants me to be, but it isn't. I can't do it, and I don't want to anymore. And I can see he isn't happy with the real me." Savannah frowned. "Does any of this make sense?"

"Somewhat." Philip smiled.

"If everything was the way I wanted, you and I would live in the same town. Philip, this isn't fair that we've just met and now have to say good-bye."

"Savannah . . ." Philip paused.

"What?"

"It's just . . . n-nothing." He shook his head.

"I should probably head back to the hostel. Especially since Shakespeare isn't going to show up!"

Philip laughed and hugged Savannah. "What are you doing tomorrow?"

"Tomorrow we all go to Warwick Castle—it's mandatory. Maybe you can come by tomorrow night?"

"I have to work; I can't get out of it."

"Well, the next day we leave for London."

Holding her by the shoulders, Philip tilted her head up toward him. "We'll figure something out, don't worry. If we both want to be with each other enough, it will work out."

Tears welled up in Savannah's eyes, and she nodded. "I hope you're right," she whispered.

They sat quietly with their arms wrapped around each other, then kissed each other once again.

Philip cleared his throat. "Uh-hum, time to pack it up, right."

Together they gathered everything and loaded it back into the wagon. When they reached the hostel, Philip walked Savannah down the drive to the back window, where her room was.

Gently, Savannah knocked on the window. Thea didn't answer right away.

"I don't understand. Her bed is right next to the window, and she's a light sleeper," Savannah whispered.

"Knock a little harder," Philip recommended. Savannah knocked again and waited. There was no response. "Try the other window," he suggested.

They walked around and knocked at the second window in the room, but no one answered.

"Maybe she didn't lock the front door behind me," Savannah said, knowing it was her only hope. They walked to the front and tried the door. It was locked. Savannah sighed. She was in big trouble now.

"Maybe you knocked too quietly," Philip offered. They went to the back again, and Savannah knocked as loudly as possible. Thea still didn't appear at the window.

"What am I going to do? I have to get in!" Savannah whispered. "If Chiochi finds out that I left . . ."

"Knock at another window?" Philip suggested.

"I don't know whose window is whose, and if I wake up Ms. Martin or Chiochi, that will be the end of any fun on this trip for me."

"Then the only other option is to come to my house. You can sleep in my sister's room—she's

130

away," Philip hastily explained. "We'll have to get back early in the morning before anyone wakes up. Ginnie, the cook here, is a friend of my family's. She'll let us in."

Savannah looked at him doubtfully.

"It will work, Savannah," he assured her. "Besides, what other choice do we have?"

"We?" Savannah echoed.

"Of course. We're in this together." Philip grinned at her. "This is an adventure—that's what you wanted, remember?"

Savannah laughed. "Philip, you're the greatest. Let's go. I just hope your parents won't mind."

"They're pretty easygoing. They'll probably be thrilled to have a houseguest," Philip told her.

After putting the wagon away and Godiva back in the small pasture behind his house, they silently entered Heart's Ease.

"Careful of the second stair," Philip whispered. "It always creaks."

"Is that you, Philip?" a woman's voice called from the kitchen.

Savannah and Philip froze at the sound of his mother's voice and stared at each other silently. Smiling weakly at Savannah, Philip answered, "Yes, Mum, I'm home."

"And who do you have with you?" Mrs. Wescott asked, coming into the living room. She was a tall woman, and she had her son's golden brown hair.

"This is Savannah Wheeler. You remember, I told you about her. Savannah, my mum," Philip introduced them.

131

"How do you do, Mrs. Wescott," Savannah said, offering her hand to Philip's mother. "I know this all looks very strange, but there is a simple explanation. I was locked out of the hostel, and Philip very kindly offered me a place to stay here. I hope that's all right with you."

Mrs. Wescott laughed softly. "It is perfectly fine with me. My daughter Anne is away, and you can stay in her room. That is what you had in mind, isn't it, Philip?"

"Of course it is, Mum," Philip answered, now smiling openly. "We just came in quietly because we didn't want to disturb you."

"I won't even ask what you two were doing out so late. I'm sure Savannah's teachers wouldn't want to know."

Savannah paled. "Please don't tell them. I-I'm not supposed to be out of the hostel. It's just that—"

"It's all right, Savannah. You can trust my mum," Philip assured her.

"Your da's asleep, so be quiet when you go upstairs. Give her enough towels, Philip," Mrs. Wescott directed her son. "Good night, Savannah. I will see you in the morning."

Silently they climbed the stairs, and Philip opened a door at the end of the hallway.

"This is Anne's room," Philip said, turning on a light. It was a small room with a sloping ceiling, lace curtains at the windows, and blue-flowered wallpaper.

"It's lovely," Savannah gasped, sitting on the four-poster bed.

"The bathroom is to your right, and I'm down the hall, on the other side of my parents' room. I'll come wake you up at five and drive you over. That should be early enough."

"Thanks, Philip."

"This is the least I could do! It's partly my fault you got locked out of the hostel. Shakespeare should have appeared earlier than he did," he joked.

"Yeah, but I'd never have believed your story if you hadn't said midnight," Savannah teased him.

"Good night, Savannah," Philip said softly, closing the door behind him.

Alone in the room, Savannah twirled around before flopping down on the bed. She was exhausted—but happier than she'd been this whole trip.

Chapter Thirteen

Savannah woke to a light knocking on the door. Startled, she looked around at the unfamiliar room.

"Savannah?" Philip whispered. "Wake up. It's six o'clock."

She jumped out of bed, her feet landing on the cold floor. "I'm up, Philip. I'll be ready in ten minutes." She quickly put on the clothes she had worn the night before and combed her hair with her fingers.

She met Philip in the hallway and smiled at the sight of him; his hair was going in all directions, his shirt was misbuttoned, and he looked half-asleep.

"It's later than I planned. I slept through the alarm. Sorry," Philip apologized.

"It's okay. I'm sure everything will be all right."

"And my parents want to say good-bye." Philip sighed wearily. "They're in the kitchen."

They went downstairs and into the kitchen,

where Mr. and Mrs. Wescott were already dressed and drinking tea.

"Well, Savannah, we meet under another strange set of circumstances," Mr. Wescott said.

"Yes, sir," Savannah replied uncertainly. She didn't know if he was annoyed or just making a comment. "Thank you both for letting me stay here."

"No problem, dear. I hope you don't get into too much trouble," Mrs. Wescott said. "I think you'd better get going before it gets really late."

"Use the car, Philip, not the wagon!" Philip's father called out as they left the house.

Savannah shivered in the cold, damp morning air and breathed in deeply, looking at the moon, which still cast pale light over the house. "Nothing can go wrong," she predicted cheerfully, despite her worries about meeting up with Mr. Chiochi.

Philip quickly started the car and headed out toward the hostel. "I'm going to see if someone can take part of my shift at the pub tonight. I might be able to get away for a little while. If not, I'll be there early tomorrow morning to say good-bye. All right?"

"I don't want to say good-bye," Savannah moaned.

Philip opened his mouth as if to say something, and then immediately shut it again.

Before she wanted to, Savannah saw the drive leading to the hostel. Philip parked the car halfway down the drive, and together they walked around the back to the kitchen. Philip knocked gently on the door, and the overweight cook quickly opened it.

"Philip Wescott! What are you doing here at this hour? And who do you have with you?" Ginnie demanded.

"Shh. Ginnie, this is Savannah. Savannah, Ginnie," Philip said as he and Savannah entered the kitchen. "Savannah was locked out last night and has to get back to her room."

"Come in. I would hurry, miss. I think there are some folks who are awake," Ginnie warned her.

"Thanks so much, Ginnie. Philip, I hope I'll see you tonight," Savannah said, kissing him before she turned to leave. She practically ran right into Mr. Chiochi, Ms. Martin, and a sleepy Thea, all three still in their pajamas and bathrobes, walking into the kitchen.

"I-I-I . . . Mr. Ch-chiochi," Savannah stuttered, her face turning bright red. "G-good m-morning, Ms. Martin."

"Savannah, where have you been all night?" Ms. Martin demanded, obviously furious and worried.

"I . . ."

"I woke up this morning hearing Elaine screaming that you were dead! It's not the way I like to wake up," Ms. Martin continued.

"We are waiting for your explanation, Ms. Wheeler."

"I-I'm sorry. I didn't think—"

"You never do!" Mr. Chiochi shouted.

Savannah felt tears well up in her eyes.

137

"Savannah, I am disappointed in you," Ms. Martin said quietly. Somehow getting a lecture from her was more upsetting to Savannah than listening to Mr. Chiochi's hysterics. "I want to hear your full explanation now."

"It's my fault, Ms. Martin," Philip interrupted.

"Again, this is your fault, young man?" Mr. Chiochi asked skeptically.

"Yes, sir," Philip replied gravely. Savannah had to stifle a giggle; it was hard to take Philip seriously with his hair a mess and his shirt misbuttoned. "I convinced Savannah that Shakespeare's ghost appeared at midnight during a full moon, especially on May Day. We stayed out late last night to see him."

"You *what*?" Ms. Martin couldn't hold back a laugh.

Savanna heard Ginnie chuckle under her breath as the cook continued her preparations for the morning oatmeal.

Philip smiled. "Yes, I know it sounds absurd in the daylight. But I figured this would intrigue Savannah. I even got a couple of my father's friends to back me up on it," Philip finished smoothly.

"This is the most ridiculous thing I've ever heard," Mr. Chiochi said. "And it's not funny, Ms. Martin."

"I know," she answered, still laughing. "But I can definitely imagine your falling for it, Savannah. You know Savannah well, Philip."

"Mr. Chiochi, Ms. Martin, I don't want you blaming Philip," Savannah began. "I knew I

138

wasn't supposed to leave the hostel, no matter how tempting it was."

"Don't worry, Savannah, I don't blame him," Ms. Martin assured her. "He may have invited you, but it was you who chose to accept, and you did know it was wrong."

"What did you do after you saw this ghost?" Mr. Chiochi asked.

Savannah looked quickly at Thea, trying to discern what she had already told them. Getting Thea into trouble was not part of her plan.

"Ms. Wheeler, I'm waiting. And don't look at Ms. Tomaselli for collaboration—we want the truth," Mr. Chiochi insisted.

"This is all my fault, Mr. Chiochi," Savannah admitted. "I don't want anyone else getting into trouble for something I've done."

"Don't worry, Ms. Wheeler, you will receive the punishment you merit, as will the others who agreed to enter this charade with you," Mr. Chiochi said, looking at Thea. "I am still waiting for your explanation."

"After we left Ann Hathaway's house, we came back here," Savannah answered in a quiet voice.

"*And?*" Mr. Chiochi prompted.

Savannah looked at Thea again for a clue as to what she had told them, but she couldn't tell from the expression on Thea's face.

Taking a deep breath, Savannah continued. "I had hoped to sneak back in through the window in my room. But it was locked. So was the front door."

"Who was supposed to let you back in?" Ms. Martin asked.

"No one," Savannah answered, holding her breath. "I guess I didn't realize the window was locked, or it relocked itself somehow. I was too excited about seeing Shakespeare's ghost."

Thea smiled slightly—enough to let Savannah know she had answered correctly.

"Then what, Savannah?" Ms. Martin asked.

"We went back to Philip's house, and I slept there."

"You what?" Mr. Chiochi cried, his hand slamming down on the wooden kitchen table.

"Sir, it's not what you think," Philip protested immediately. "Savannah stayed in my sister's room, and I was in mine. Honest."

Blushing, Savannah added, "Mr. Chiochi, please. Philip's parents were right there. I stayed in the nicest room, with a four-poster bed, lace curtains, and the loveliest, most English wallpaper—"

"Savannah, I'm glad you enjoyed it," Ms. Martin said dryly, "but that is not the point here."

"I'm sorry, Ms. Martin. It was all so totally innocent, except that I knew I wasn't supposed to leave the grounds," Savannah quickly added when she saw Mr. Chiochi's face about to turn a deeper shade of red.

"I want to call your home, young man, to confirm this," Mr. Chiochi said. "We will go the hostel office and call them from here."

Philip smiled reassuringly at Savannah, and the small group followed Mr. Chiochi out the kitchen and down the hallway. Other students were already up and coming down for breakfast. Not wanting to see anyone, Savannah stared straight ahead.

The five of them crowded into the small hostel office, and Philip rang up his home. After a few moments he said, "Da, hi. Sorry to bother you, but I need you to talk to Mr. Chiochi, the man in charge of Savannah's trip. Thanks." Philip handed the phone over to Mr. Chiochi.

"Mr. Wescott, hello. Yes, this is Mr. Chiochi, and I just want to confirm what happened last night." Mr. Chiochi paused as he listened to Philip's father. "Yes, she is a bit flighty and too old to believe in ghosts."

"Yes, I see," Mr. Chiochi continued after a long pause. "Thank you very much for letting her stay in your home. I hope you weren't put out. I'll tell him. Good-bye, Mr. Wescott." Mr. Chiochi hung up the phone and turned to Philip. "Your father is quite a gentleman. He wants you home immediately. We are leaving Stratford tomorrow," Mr. Chiochi told him. "You are not under my jurisdiction, Mr. Wescott, but I would be most displeased if I saw you around here again."

"Mr. Chiochi, you can't—" Savannah started to protest.

"Ms. Wheeler, I don't want to hear it," Mr. Chiochi said sharply. He turned back to Philip. "Do you understand, young man?"

Philip nodded mutely.

"Mr. Chiochi, I believe we can give Savannah

and Philip a few moments of privacy to say good-bye," Ms. Martin offered.

The two adults and Thea left the room. Savannah stared at Philip, tears filling her eyes, and then ran to him.

Philip wrapped his arms around her and stroked her hair. "Don't worry, Savannah. I'll be back tonight, even if I have to storm the battlements."

Savannah's giggles were muffled by his sweater. She lifted her head and smiled. "Thanks for helping me out with Chiochi."

"A Wescott is always true to his lady fair."

Ms. Martin knocked on the door and opened it. "I'm sorry, Philip, you'll have to go. Savannah, go into the dining room for your breakfast. You'll have time to wash up before we go out today."

Savannah hugged Philip again and hurried out of the room. She didn't want to look back. Before going into the dining room, she ducked into a small room off the hallway to control her tears. In just a few short days Philip had become as important to her as her family and Thea, and now she would never see him again! *It isn't fair!* she thought to herself. *And now I can't even spend one last day with him!*

Knowing Mr. Chiochi would come looking for her if she didn't show up for breakfast, Savannah wiped her eyes and left the small room. In the noisy dining room, she nonchalantly walked over to get a bowl of oatmeal and heard the entire room become quiet. Then she heard Thea loudly ask Emma to pass the salt, and the room filled with noise once again.

Ginnie was filling the serving bowl with more hot porridge. She shook her head and murmured, "Young love . . ."

Savannah tried to smile, but her chin shook slightly as she felt the tears starting again.

"Sorry, dearie. I'm sure it will all work out," Ginnie assured her before leaving for the kitchen.

Savannah turned around and saw the whole room staring at her.

"Savannah, over here!" Thea called, patting the chair next to her. Savannah sat down at a table with Thea, Emma, Elaine, and Danielle.

"So what happened? What went on last night?" Danielle asked, once Savannah had eaten a spoonful of oatmeal.

"Maybe she doesn't want to talk about it, Danielle," Thea said.

"You should have seen Chiochi and Ms. Martin when they came out of the office," Elaine said. "He was steaming!"

"Elaine," Thea warned.

"I want to know what happened last night, Thea," Savannah said. "Didn't you hear me knocking?"

"I'm really sorry, Savannah. Elaine insisted on switching beds because she said Emma rolled too much and she couldn't sleep. I didn't want to tell her where you were," Thea said, staring significantly at Elaine. "But I couldn't think of a good reason why I couldn't move. I was sure I would hear the knock no matter what, but I must have been more tired than usual from being up so early. I was totally zonked. I'm sorry."

"Don't worry, you tried. I just should have had a Plan B. I definitely want to know what happened this morning, though, Elaine," Savannah demanded.

"I'm sorry you got into trouble, Savannah, but how was I to know you were up to some new stunt?" Elaine primly pointed out. "When we got up and you were the only one not awake—"

"I tried to stop her, Savannah," Thea interrupted.

"I nudged you awake, and you didn't respond," Elaine said.

Emma laughed. "So she screamed!"

"Anyone with half a brain could see that there were pillows under the covers. Ms. Martin noticed that right away," Thea added, giggling.

"Well, I thought that you were dead or something," Elaine continued, flipping her hair back over her shoulder. "Ms. Martin came running in and pulled off the covers, and that's when she discovered you weren't in your bed."

"Ms. Martin grabbed me, and we went to see Mr. Chiochi," Thea explained. "We heard voices in the kitchen, and there you were. I'm sorry it all got so messed up."

"Thea, it's not your fault. I'm so glad I didn't tell them that you were supposed to let me back in!" Savannah finished eating her oatmeal. "I wonder what they're going to do to me."

"What happened with Philip? I told you he was a cutie," Emma reminded her.

"Oh, nothing and everything. He's wonderful! You guys were right about that. And now I'll never see him again."

"Ms. Wheeler and Ms. Tomaselli, I want to see you both in the main room," Mr. Chiochi said, standing at the end of their table.

"Yes, sir." The two girls rose, and Savannah quickly scanned the room for Greg. When she caught his eye, he purposely looked away.

"Girls, I am disappointed in both of you," Mr. Chiochi began once they were seated on the couch.

"Please, Mr. Chiochi, Thea had nothing to do with this," Savannah repeated.

"Ms. Wheeler, no matter what you may think, I am not a fool. If one of you is involved in something, you can bet that the other one is not far behind." He paused to take a breath. "I am also not an ogre. At first, I wanted to stop both of you from going on the trip to Warwick today, but I realized that was too harsh. It also wasn't fair for me to forbid you to see your friend. I've decided that you may call him tonight."

"Oh, Mr. Chiochi, thank you!" Savannah responded passionately, giving him a hug.

"Ms. Wheeler, you'll have to learn to control your outbursts," Mr. Chiochi said sternly.

"Yes, Mr. Chiochi," she answered demurely.

"I am not happy with what you did. I am responsible for you girls, although you seem to forget that fact whenever it suits your needs. If anything happens to you, it's my fault." Mr. Chiochi was silent, and for the first time Savannah realized he was uncomfortable.

He cleared his throat and turned away from the girls. "I can understand if you don't want to answer this next question, Ms. Wheeler. But I have to ask it."

Savannah bit her lip. "What is it, Mr. Chiochi?"

"Did you see anything of Shakespeare's ghost?" he asked sheepishly.

The two girls looked at each other and burst out laughing.

Mr. Chiochi turned a bright shade of pink.

"Oh, Mr. Chiochi, I'm sorry," Savannah finally said when she caught her breath, "and you certainly aren't an ogre!"

Chapter Fourteen

After getting changed, Savannah wandered to the back of the hostel. She knew she needed to be by herself and think things out.

She stopped dead when she saw Elaine and Greg sitting very close to each other on the stone bench. "Oh!" she said softly. Elaine and Greg turned around.

"Savannah!" Elaine exclaimed, jumping up. "I-I'll leave you two alone." Giving Greg and Savannah one last look, she quickly walked away.

Savannah stared straight at Greg. Before she could lose courage, she said, "Greg, we need to talk to each other, now."

"What is it, Savannah?" he asked.

" 'What is it?' I can't believe you can ask that!" she practically shouted.

"Don't yell at me!"

"What else shouldn't I do? And why did you avoid me all through breakfast? Some friend you are!" she snorted.

"What do you expect from me? You leave the

hostel after curfew and then spend the night with some stranger!"

"Ooh, you make me so angry! You have no idea what I did! You never asked! You assumed everything from whatever rumors you over-heard," Savannah stormed, pacing angrily in front of Greg.

"Maybe so, but did I say anything that wasn't true? Isn't that what happened?" Greg argued.

"What if it is? What's so terrible about what I've done?"

"You made me look like a fool!" Greg finally shouted.

Savannah stared at him. "What are you talking about?"

Greg raked his hand through his hair. "You really don't know, do you? First, you break the rules and go out after curfew. And to top it off, you're with this other guy, and then you spend the whole night out of the hostel. Everyone knows we are—or *were*—a couple, and there you are, out with another guy, doing dumb things."

"Don't you dare make me feel bad for being with Philip," Savannah warned. "You and Elaine seem to have gotten pretty cozy."

Greg reddened. "That's beside the point. You're my girlfriend; what you do reflects on me."

"And what you do reflects on me."

"I don't do anything weird."

"Yes, you do," Savannah replied sadly. "You don't like me just for me—you like me for who you want me to be. You ignore me when I've done something you think is wrong—a real friend doesn't do that. You get angry at me and scold me and treat me like a baby. I know people who would think that's weird. And all I've done is defend you to everyone."

"I don't embarrass you," Greg protested.

"Yes, you do," Savannah said slowly. "Every time you've treated me like a fool or a baby, I've been embarrassed."

"You're doing it again. You're changing things to fit your strange way of seeing things," Greg said accusingly.

"And you're criticizing me again! Greg, do you know that you never even asked me if I was your girlfriend—you just assumed it?" Savannah said, getting angry again.

"I didn't hear you protesting," Greg said smugly.

"I was spending all my time trying to be the girl you wanted me to be," Savannah admitted. "But you never gave me any credit for that—you just told me everything I was doing was wrong!"

"If you did things right, I wouldn't *have* to. If you acted like girls are supposed to act, we wouldn't be fighting now."

Savannah slapped her arms against her sides in disgust. "I can't believe I fell for you!"

"I can't believe I ever thought you could be anything but what you are—an immature nut!" Greg cried.

"That's it! I thought we could still be friends, but now I sincerely doubt it." Savannah twirled around and headed for the front of the hostel.

Abruptly she stopped, turned back again, and smiled sweetly. "For someone who's supposedly so mature, I'm surprised you had to resort to such infantile behavior as name-calling, Mr. Edwards."

Savannah turned again and calmly walked up the path. By the time she reached her room, she was grinning.

"Is this the same Savannah I just heard screaming?" Thea asked.

Savannah laughed. "Was I that loud? Sorry. I just realized I feel free—totally free for the first time on this trip. I don't have to pretend anything anymore."

"Welcome back, Savannah Wheeler! I've missed you!" Thea said, hugging her friend.

"So what new adventures should we have today?" Savannah asked.

Chapter Fifteen

Walking slowly down the hallway to her room, Savannah trailed her finger along the wooden wall. Madeleine came out of the room she shared with the other girls and glanced inquiringly at Savannah, who shook her head no.

When she entered her room, Elaine, Thea, and Emma stopped packing and raised their heads.

"The line's still busy," Savannah told them with a sigh. She walked over to her backpack and continued to sort through her clothes, getting ready for their early departure for London in the morning.

"He said he would say good-bye to you, and he will," Emma declared firmly.

"It's almost seven o'clock. Soon the doors will be locked. Even though Chiochi said I could see him, he won't like Philip sneaking around the hostel," Savannah mused. "I wish I'd been able to get through to him at the pub and tell him it's okay for him to come by!" she exclaimed, throwing her clothes into her backpack.

"Torturing your clothes isn't going to help," Thea teased. "He said he had to work tonight—he's probably on his way."

"Be realistic, Savannah. Either he'll come or he won't," Elaine said as she zipped her suitcase closed. "Worrying about it isn't going to help."

"Shut up, Elaine. You don't know anything about it!" Thea exploded.

"This is my room as well as anybody else's. I don't have to be quiet," she pouted. "Besides, what's the big deal about Philip?"

There was a moment of silence as all three girls stared at Elaine.

"Well," Savannah said, forcing a bright smile, "it's not like he's the only boy on earth. Besides, after tonight, I won't ever see him again." Methodically, Savannah refolded her clothes properly and placed them neatly in her backpack.

"Uh-oh, Savannah's really upset if she's being neat," Thea commented, watching her friend carefully.

"No, I'm just trying to be realistic like Elaine suggested," she answered calmly.

"I hope you're not really mad at me," Elaine said when she saw how quiet Savannah was.

"Why would I be?"

"Well, if it weren't for me, you and Philip wouldn't have gotten caught this morning."

Savannah looked her straight in the eye. "I'm sure you didn't mean to get me in trouble."

"And . . ." Elaine began hesitantly, looking very uncomfortable. "Well . . . I'm sort of . . . I mean . . ."

"Spit it out, Lacey," Thea insisted, looking disgusted.

"Well, Greg and I are going out now," Elaine said in a rush.

Savannah couldn't help herself; she burst out laughing. Without knowing why, the other two girls began laughing too.

Finally Savannah caught her breath and wiped the tears from her eyes as Elaine stared at her. "Thanks, Elaine, that's the best laugh I've had in a while. You can keep Greg, with my blessings. He's . . . well, I always thought you and he were better suited to each other anyway."

"Is everything all right in here?" Ms. Martin was standing at the door, staring at the three girls who were sprawled on the floor, clutching their stomachs.

"We're fine, Ms. Martin," Elaine answered stiffly.

"Just a little giddy—jet lag, you know," Thea added. The three girls burst out laughing again, and Ms. Martin shook her head and closed the door.

When their breathing returned to normal, the three girls continued packing as Elaine watched.

"Did you hear that?" Elaine suddenly whispered.

The three girls stopped packing and listened.

"I don't hear anything," Emma said.

"Turn off the light," Savannah whispered as she scrambled over the suitcases and backpacks to look out each window. "I don't see anything," she said.

"I still hear a rustling noise," Elaine insisted.

"So do I," Thea agreed.

Elaine moved closer to the window near Thea's bed. Suddenly she screamed.

The door swung open and Ms. Martin stood there in the dim light from the hallway. "What is going on? Why are you in the dark?" she demanded, switching on the light.

"Sorry, Ms. Martin, it was my fault," Elaine said. "I was startled."

Ms. Martin raised her eyebrows. "Again? By what? What is out there?"

"We were looking at the stars, Ms. Martin," Savannah began.

"Yes?"

"One last time, you know, in the English countryside."

"And it was a shooting star!" Thea exclaimed.

"It scared me. I wasn't expecting it," Elaine said, a serious look on her face.

Ms. Martin looked at the four girls, and they calmly looked back at her. "It's hard to believe, but you girls are actually more trouble than the boys. You four especially. I don't want to hear anything else coming from this room, do you understand?"

"Yes, Ms. Martin," Savannah said obediently.

"Good night," Thea said as Ms. Martin closed the door behind her.

Once the door was closed, Emma hit the lights again, and they all resumed their places by the windows.

"Why did you scream, Elaine?" Thea asked, shaking her head. "What is your problem?"

"I saw a face staring at me."

"It must be Philip!" Savannah exclaimed, opening her window. "Philip, is that you?" she whispered loudly.

Philip's face popped up immediately. "This place is more difficult to break into than the Tower," Philip complained as he hoisted himself up on the ledge and into their room. "I've been out there knocking, but you all were laughing so hard, you didn't hear me. And then when you screamed," he said, pointing to Elaine, "you scared me so much I almost didn't try again."

"How are you doing?" Savannah asked shyly. Now that he was actually here, she felt uncomfortable.

"Not bad," he answered, seeming nervous himself. "But I don't have much time. Tim can only cover for me another half hour. My parents are angry with me. Not with you, they like you," Philip quickly said when he saw Savannah's stricken face. "It was the old 'I should have known better.' If they find out that I came here tonight, that would be it for me."

"Well, I think we need to wash up for bed, girls, don't you?" Thea said, getting her towel.

"Huh?" Elaine asked.

"Wash up? Leave the room for a while!" Thea hinted, grabbing Elaine's towel and hand and pulling her toward the door.

"Oh, right. Nice seeing you again, Philip," Elaine said, and the three girls left, closing the door behind them.

Once Savannah and Philip were alone in the room, they rushed into each other's arms.

"Oh, Philip, I thought I'd never see you again!" Savannah whispered.

"I told you I would see you tonight, no matter what."

"All I could think about was that I never gave you my address in Boston," Savannah said, sitting on her bed.

"Savannah, don't worry so much. We can see each other again." Philip sat down beside her.

"What do you mean? I leave for London tomorrow."

"I know. And I'll be there the next day," Philip informed her.

"What are you talking about?"

"I didn't want to say anything earlier because I wasn't sure, but I'm going to London to stay with some relatives for a week. So I can see you there. Of course, we'll have to sneak visits."

"No, we won't. After you left today, Mr. Chiochi said that he was wrong to forbid our seeing each other. I've been calling the pub for over three hours to tell you! But the line was busy all night," Savannah explained.

"You mean I slunk around in the bushes for nothing?" Philip laughed.

"Not for nothing. For your lady love," Savannah joked.

Philip knelt on the floor and held her hand in his. "As usual, you are right, Lady Savannah. Getting savaged by thorny bushes, getting my eardrums busted by Elaine's shrill voice, scraping my knees climbing through a window . . . it all means nothing if I can kneel—on my bloody knees—beside my lady."

"Philip!" Savannah exclaimed, pulling him to his feet. "Are you really bleeding?" She examined his pants and realized he was teasing. Stamping her foot and looking up at his laughing face, she said, "I am never going to believe another word you say!"

He held her hands and looked at her gravely. "Believe this, Savannah Wheeler. I will see you in London in two nights. And that won't be the last time, either."

A light knock at the door interrupted Savannah's response. Thea opened the door and stuck her head in. "Sorry, but Ms. Martin was getting suspicious again." She entered the room with Emma and Elaine behind her.

"That's okay. I have to leave anyway," Philip said. "Where are you guys staying in London?"

"The Cosmo Bed and Breakfast at Bloomsbury Square," Thea said.

"I'll be there in two nights, Savannah. See you soon." Philip kissed her lightly on the lips,

157

waved good-bye to the others, and climbed out the window.

Savannah ran to the window, blew him a kiss, then leaned against the sill. "This is the most romantic thing that has ever happened to me." She sighed dramatically. "I don't know how I'll live through the next two days."

"You'll find a way, buckaroo," Thea said, punching Savannah lightly on the shoulder.

Chapter Sixteen

Two nights later, Ms. Martin returned with the class from a play to find a very disappointed and very subdued Savannah sitting in a red velvet chair in the lobby of the bed-and-breakfast. After saying good night to everyone, Ms. Martin returned to the sitting room.

"What happened, Savannah? Didn't Philip show up tonight?" she asked gently.

Savannah shook her head, tears filling her eyes. "You don't think something bad happened to him, do you?"

"Oh, no, dear," Ms. Martin said. "Do you know where he's staying? We could call him."

Savannah shook her head and gulped. "I only know he's staying with relatives somewhere in London."

"We can call Stratford if you like and ask his parents," Ms. Martin suggested.

"Oh no, Ms. Martin, I can't. Maybe he just decided he didn't want to see me anymore. . . ." Savannah began weeping again.

"Do you really believe that?" her teacher asked.

"Well, I guess not. But after all, I will be leaving in a few days. I just sat here all night, hoping nothing bad had happened to him."

"Well, if you don't hear from him by tomorrow when we get back from our day out, I think we'd better call Stratford. Okay?" Ms. Martin said, lifting Savannah's teary face. Savannah tried to smile, but couldn't. She just nodded her agreement.

"What a glorious day it's been!" Thea sighed as the whole class walked back to the bed-and-breakfast from the tube stop.

"Yes, it was," Savannah agreed absently.

"Oh, Savannah, I'm sorry," Thea quickly said.

"Don't be. It was a great day—the Tower, the crown jewels, a ride down the Thames, Saint Paul's Cathedral, and then a concert at the Royal Albert Hall. I even forgot about Philip every so often," Savannah said. "Either there will be a message from him when we get back, or there won't."

Thea put her arm around her friend and squeezed lightly. "I'm sure there'll be a message for you, and I'm sure he's okay."

Savannah smiled wanly at her friend and shrugged.

Silently they walked with the rest of the class. As they got nearer to the small inn, Savannah could feel her heart pounding harder and harder. Murmuring under her breath, she said, "Please be okay, Philip. Please be there."

When they entered the bed-and-breakfast, Savannah waited for Ms. Martin, who checked to see if there were any messages at the front desk. She came back out to the hallway and shook her head no.

Savannah felt her heart sink. "Ms. Martin, do you mind if I sit up alone for a while?" she asked, fighting back tears. "I just need to think."

"Savannah, we can call his parents," Ms. Martin reminded her.

"No," she stated emphatically. "I want to write a letter to him—I think that will be best."

"All right. I'll tell Mr. Chiochi where you are."

"Thanks, Ms. Martin." Trudging heavily, Savannah entered the dark sitting room and felt around for a light switch. Remembering that there were only lamps, she put out her hand, searching for one of the little tables.

As she reached for a lamp, she felt something soft and warm—something alive. And when she heard a grunt, Savannah screamed and ran out of the room, knocking over a chair on the way.

The two teachers and some of her classmates immediately came running down the stairs.

"What is it, Ms. Wheeler?" Mr. Chiochi demanded.

"I-I f-felt s-something ghastly," Savannah panted, trying to get the words out.

She saw Mr. Chiochi's worried frown turn into a smile.

"I think that 'ghastly' thing is behind you now," he said.

Savannah slowly turned and saw a sleepy and

shocked Philip, rubbing the sleep out of his eyes. "This is the most dangerous relationship I've ever been involved in," he complained as he squinted against the light in the hallway.

"Philip!" Savannah rushed to hug him, then stopped midway. "Where have you been? You've had me so worried!"

"I—"

"I can't believe what you've put me through! I'm furious with you!" Savannah continued, not even giving Philip a chance to answer.

"Well, I—"

"How could you have forgotten to come!"

"Ms. Wheeler—" Mr. Chiochi tried to break in.

"I should never speak to you again!" Savannah raged, ignoring Philip's attempts to answer her. "I imagined you were dead. I th—"

"Savannah!" Mr. Chiochi yelled.

Savannah stopped midsentence. She turned slowly and faced Mr. Chiochi, her mouth open. "That's the second time you've called me Savannah," she said, amazed. "I didn't think you knew my first name."

"It was the only way to get you to be quiet! I think this young man is trying to say something to you. Why don't you two go into the sitting room and talk—but only for a few minutes. I expect to hear you coming up those stairs very shortly." Mr. Chiochi turned to go back up the stairs and noticed for the first time that all the students were watching the scene.

"The rest of you get up to your rooms now!" he ordered.

Slowly everyone left, leaving only Philip and Savannah in the hallway.

"I guess we should go into the sitting room," Philip offered tentatively.

Savannah turned on a small lamp and picked up the chair she had knocked over. She giggled. "I'm surprised Mr. and Mrs. Quinn didn't wake up from all this racket."

"They wear earplugs," Philip said.

"How do you know?"

"I've been waiting here for hours for you. I also called a number of times during the day, but you were always out. Mr. and Mrs. Quinn are practically my best friends now."

"Oh, Philip!" Savannah cried, putting her arms around him. "I was so worried about you. What happened?" she asked, looking up at him.

"Well, it's sort of a long and involved story, and Mr. Chiochi did say we only had a few minutes. Maybe I'd just better come back tomorrow," he teased.

"Philip!" Savannah warned. "Tell me everything now." She pulled him to the sofa, where they sat down.

"Well, okay, since you insist," Philip said, settling next to her on the couch, his arm around her waist. "I came to London to see my aunt and uncle, because I had an interview for a university I've been wanting to go to for a long time. I've already taken all the exams, but yesterday was my interview. It kept getting postponed, which is why I was never sure I was coming to London when you were. I wanted to tell you about the possibility of my being here when you first mentioned it, but I . . ."

"But what?"

Philip blushed. "I didn't know how you would react when a total stranger wanted to follow you from city to city. I thought I should wait a bit." Savannah grinned and kissed him on the cheek.

"Ms. Wheeler, I must insist that you come up now. It's late!" Mr. Chiochi called from upstairs.

"I'll be right there," Savannah replied. "Go on with your story," she told Philip.

"Anyway, this Mr. Browne kept making the interview later and later because of his business. Finally, he saw me at five o'clock."

"And?"

"Well, we were interrupted by a few business calls from the States, so he decided to take me out to dinner—and we ended up staying out until midnight talking, which is why I couldn't make it here last night." Philip leaned his head against Savannah's. "I didn't want to do anything like interrupt him or say I had to make a phone call, because everything was riding on this interview."

"And?" Savannah asked.

"He liked me. He said he hadn't laughed that much in years."

"I'm sure he thought you were more than funny."

"Well, yes, but the school already has the results from all the exams. This was a more personal thing. And I think he felt bad because of all the difficulties we had just getting to see each other," Philip explained.

"So, did you get in?"

"Yes!" Philip exclaimed.

"Philip!" Savannah squealed. "That's great! I'm so glad it's good news."

"Ms. Wheeler!" Mr. Chiochi warned from the top of the stairs.

"I'm just saying good night now, Mr. Chiochi. I'll be there in a minute!" Savannah promised.

"I'm sorry I wasn't here," Philip said.

"That's okay—you're safe and you got into the school you wanted. You'll have to write and tell me how it is. Please promise you'll write."

"Well, I thought I would call you."

"That would be great!" Savannah said with a smile.

"And maybe see you every so often," Philip said slowly.

"What are you talking about?"

"Well, I'm not great at geography, but isn't Harvard in Bos—"

"Philip Wescott! You're rotten!" Savannah exclaimed, hitting him on the arm.

"I thought you would be pleased," Philip protested as he tried to evade her blows.

"I can't believe it! When?" Savannah asked.

"I'll be there in the middle of August."

"That's not for another four and a half months," Savannah wailed, counting on her fingers. "But it's better than I ever imagined," she concluded happily.

Philip clasped her hands in his. "Savannah, do you know how many letters we can write in four and a half months? It will be like we've never been apart. And you can show me the real Boston."

"We can go boating on the Charles—"

"Well, maybe not boating," he joked.

"And walking along the Promenade," Savannah continued, "and we can eat cannoli in the North End and—"

"And get up to bed," Mr. Chiochi interrupted, standing in the doorway. "Ms. Wheeler—"

"Please call me Savannah," she begged, grinning.

"I'll make a bargain. I'll call you Savannah when you stay out of trouble for an entire week," Mr. Chiochi proposed, smiling.

"You drive a hard bargain. I think I'm doomed to being Ms. Wheeler through eternity. I'll just have to get used to it." Savannah turned to Philip. "I guess we have to say good night. Parting is such sweet sorrow . . . Mr. Chiochi?"

"Yes, Ms. Wheeler?" He sighed heavily.

"If Philip wants to and if he can, may he join us tomorrow?" Savannah asked.

He looked sternly at her, but slowly his face softened. "If he can stand it, he may. I want you upstairs in a minute, Ms. Wheeler. Good night, Philip," Mr. Chiochi said, leaving the room and going back upstairs.

"How come he calls *you* by your first name?" Savannah said indignantly.

166

"Let's not waste our minute talking," Philip said. He moved closer to Savannah and wrapped his arms around her.

Savannah sighed as she put her arms around Philip's neck and they kissed. "Who ever said that all good things must come to an end?"

We hope you enjoyed reading this book. If you would like to receive further information about available titles in the Bantam series, just write to the address below, with your name and address: Kim Prior, Bantam Books, 61–63 Uxbridge Road, Ealing, London W5 5SA.

If you live in Australia or New Zealand and would like more information about the series, please write to:

Sally Porter
Transworld Publishers
(Australia) Pty Ltd
15–23 Helles Avenue
Moorebank
NSW 2170
AUSTRALIA

Kiri Martin
Transworld Publishers (NZ) Ltd
Cnr. Moselle and Waipareira
Avenues
Henderson
Auckland
NEW ZEALAND

All Bantam and Young Adult books are available at your bookshop or newsagent, or can be ordered at the following address: Corgi/Bantam Books, Cash Sales Department, PO Box 11, Falmouth, Cornwall, TR10 9EN.

Please list the title(s) you would like, and send together with a cheque or postal order. You should allow for the cost of book(s) plus postage and packing charges as follows:

80p for one book
£1.00 for two books
£1.20 for three books
£1.40 for four books
Five or more books free.

Please note that payment must be made in pounds sterling; other currencies are unacceptable.

(The above applies to readers in the UK and Republic of Ireland only)

BFPO customers, please allow for the cost of the book(s) plus the following for postage and packing: 80p for the first book, and 20p for each additional copy.

Overseas customers, please allow £1.50 for postage and packing for the first book, £1.00 for the second book, and 30p for each subsequent title ordered.

First love . . . first kiss!

A terrific series that focuses firmly on that most important moment·in any girl's life – falling in love for the very
first time ever.

Available from wherever Bantam paperbacks are sold!

1. **Head Over Heels** by Susan Blake
2. **Love Song** by Suzanne Weyn
3. **Falling for You** by Carla Bracale
4. **The Perfect Couple** by Helen Santori

HE NOTICED I'M ALIVE ...
AND OTHER HOPEFUL SIGNS
by Marjorie Sharmat

' My life changed in four hours.'

Jody can hardly believe her luck when Matt Green walks into her life one evening. He's incredibly good-looking and he even seems to like her too!

But Jody's life soon starts to become horribly compli-cated. With her mother still traveling the world 'finding herself', and her father getting much too serious about Matt's mother, Jody isn't sure where she stands with Matt himself – especially as everything she says to him seems to lead to ghastly misunderstandings.

Soon Jody has to admit she's made a real mess of things with Matt. Now she can only wait for him to make a move . . .

'A light upbeat read' BOOKLIST

0 553 40105 X